Lucy Tuppins Hawaiian Adventure Series

Lucy Tuppins Hawaiian Adventure Series

The Queen's Treasure

S. R. Bell

The Queen's Treasure is a work of fiction. Names, characters, places, and incidents based on history of the Hawaiian Islands are the products of the author's imagination or are used fictitiously. Any resemblance to actual events, locales, or persons, living or dead, is entirely coincidental.

Acknowledgments: This book in the Lucy Tuppins Hawaiian Adventure Series is the first of five. I want to thank my editor, Carissa Frechette, for her willingness to help me rewrite this story; and Cynthia Dahle of Minneapolis for creating and designing the covers in the Lucy Tuppins series. And to my family and friends who let me go on and on about my little blonde haired character over the past three years. It is with their love and support that the story of a little missionary girl finally got printed (my husband Doug, Mary Aymar, Ui Goldsberry, David Crotty, Michael Palmieri, Mary Booth, Molokai, Gwen Adams, Kerry Gogan, Karen Arora, and two little boys named Oliver and Eugene).

Dedication

For my best friend, Janice Booth
whose kind heart and wisdom
led me into the magical world of
writing and helped me find my
little Lucy Tuppins.

One

The Robbery

London, April 1826

A resounding noise cut through the night – the slow clanging of a bell in the church tower right next door shook floorboards under the small girl's cot. She counted the number of times the bell rang: one, two, three, four, five, six, seven, eight, nine, ten, eleven – and with the twelfth echoing tone she knew that it was midnight. *Its only midnight?* She sighed deeply and stretched out her arms.

The night air brought a nasty chill to the room. She began to shiver and felt a droplet of moisture fall on her face. Eight year old Lucy Tuppins was tucked away in the cold, dark attic of the vicarage high above four flights of creaky wooden steps: the only available space for a one night's lodging. She sat reluctantly on a tiny cot and hugged her knees to her chest.

Just as she was about to dangle her legs over the side of the prickly mattress, she thought she heard the slow grinding turn of a doorknob from across the dark room. Suddenly and without warning, a gust of air swirled around the room making the door slam open with a vengeance. It happened so quickly that she didn't even have time to pull the blanket up over her head and hide.

"Why aren't you asleep?" groaned her father as he stood in the doorway holding a lantern.

"Papa," she replied. "It's the storm."

"I told you not to get out of bed," he scolded. "I can hear you moving around from downstairs."

"But I did as you asked and –"

"Enough with excuses," he interrupted. "Get to sleep. I'll be here at six o'clock and we will have breakfast before we head for the docks. Be sure that you are dressed and ready for the voyage."

"Yes, Papa."

Lucy watched as he pulled the door shut behind. She wished her father's words were kinder. He was a very important Bishop in the Church and he expected Lucy to be a good, well-mannered little girl all the time. She loved her father dearly, but she found living up to his standards was almost impossible.

Her mother had been kind. But Lucy's mother was dead now. She had been sick for many months, and one day she fell asleep but never woke up. Lucy had been seven years old and her father tried to comfort the little girl by saying, "You know that your mother is watching over you and you have nothing to fear." And that was the last time he talked about her mother. Lucy was sure that her father missed Mrs. Tuppins too, but he never said a word about it to his daughter. She missed her mother a lot.

Earlier that evening, Bishop Tuppins and his daughter had arrived at the Diocese Vicarage in London. They were about to leave England for a missionary assignment half way across the world. When Lucy asked why, her father told her that he wanted to leave all the memories behind them. But Lucy didn't want to forget her mother or her home in the Cotswold. And she especially didn't want to go live on an island in the middle of the Pacific Ocean.

Another hour had passed and the flurry of thoughts made Lucy even more restless. She felt more awake than ever before and was bored. She quietly got up off the cot and carefully crept barefooted across the cold floor to the attic window. It was so filthy she could hardly see through the glass. She put a little spit on the end of her cotton nightgown and rubbed in a circle until the dirt vanished but the buildup of soot from the chimneys lining the alley below covered the outside of the glass as well.

Lucy crawled up onto the bench beneath the sill to get a better look. She knew that the wind had calmed to a slight breeze *since the creaking* in the rafters had stopped. She stood on the tip of her toes to unhook the window latch at the top.

With her two palms, she gently pressed on the glass pane of each side of the window and they swung out over the lane beneath the night sky.

Wow, she thought to herself. She was standing high above the alley and could see a lot in the moonlight. Most little girls of eight didn't consider the dangers of leaning out a high window, and Lucy was no different. Slipping and falling didn't even cross her mind. She was focused on the rows and rows of chimneys and the rooftops of London glistening with wetness as the dark menacing clouds churned off in the distance.

In particular, she noticed an enormous building across the cobblestone pathway with carvings around all the windows. The building rose up from the ground so high that it looked like the rooftop was in the stars.

Then she remembered that upon their arrival, guards had escorted their buggy through a pair of massive iron gates. They wore red woolen jackets, large black dome shaped hats, and carried rifles. Lucy had been too busy talking to her father to consider these details earlier. It was only now that she realized the building she was in was part of the Palace where the Queen of England lived.

Suddenly a heavy crash of thunder made the thick timbers shake. She saw everyone on the lane scatter like little ants. Drops of rain came down to pellet her pale forehead, but they didn't deter her from watching the alley. It was deserted now, all except for a sentry who stood guard across the alley in front of a large wooden door.

She wondered why the man didn't get out of the rain. It was just silliness to continue standing outside the door getting drenched, even if it was to guard the Queen. She thought he could guard Her Majesty on the other side of the door just as well.

"Hello!" she cried out, waving her hands to get his attention. The sentry moved in Lucy's direction, without looking up at her. "Hello!" she tried again. But her greeting was ignored. Back and forth he continued to pace along the wall. By now her nightgown was drenched with wetness, so she gave up on the sentry and reached out to close the window. But a cry from below stopped her short.

"Halt!" the guard shouted.

She stared down through the downpour to see the hooded figure of another man exiting the large Palace door. He appeared to be carrying something, but Lucy couldn't make it out. The rain had begun to pour out of the sky even harder. It was getting difficult for her to see through the deluge.

Peering through the rain, she saw the guard rush at the hooded man. Lucy feared the guard may be no match for the intruder; who seemed bigger and more muscular. She watched them struggle and was amazed when the guard managed to push the man against the wall. She believed for a moment that the guard would win but then his opponent managed to wrestle the rifle from him and knock him down. Lucy called out, "Stop! Stop!", but her voice was like a whisper in the raging storm.

Lucy slid off the window seat and burst through the attic door, then ran down the four flights of stairs as fast as she could. A feeling that something really bad was going to happen stirred in her gut and her heart was pounding furiously against her chest. She shouted, "Papa! Papa!" as her bare feet landed on the cold stone of the first floor. "Help, someone!" But everyone in the vicarage was fast asleep.

Within minutes, Lucy found herself in the pitch dark kitchen. Frantically, she felt around for the back door. When she found it, the door wouldn't open when she tried it. She examined the door with her hands and realized that there was a bar bolting her exit. With all her might, Lucy pushed and pushed until it finally dislodged. She shoved her shoulder into the thick oak door and it creaked open just enough for her tiny body to slip through, out into the pouring rain.

In the alley, lying in a heap and surrounded by puddles, was the palace guard she had been watching. Lucy stood over the motionless body as the rain beat down on her flushed cheeks. She didn't know what to do and wondered if he was still alive. Just as she was about to bend down and check she felt a hot breath on the back of her neck. She cautiously turned around and found herself up close to a horse's nostrils. Lucy froze in place.

The world seemed to slow for the next few tense moments. On the saddle sat a man with cold icy blue eyes, staring at her from under a hood. Without warning, the horse shoved her off balance and she fell onto the guard. Lucy hadn't felt the cold before because she was pumped up with adrenaline from all the excitement. But now she had a chill of fright shivering up her spine.

Across the alleyway, light spilled out from the vicarage kitchen door. Seeing this, the hooded man sped off into the night with his horse. Lucy was overjoyed when she saw the old housekeeper wobbling on the cobblestones. Back and forth her bosom swayed as she came close to Lucy.

"Miss Tuppins!" she called out, wrapping her arms around Lucy. "What are you doing out here? Your mother will be very upset."

"My mother is dead," Lucy replied with a trembling voice, pushing the wet blonde curls out of her eyes.

"Oh!" said the old lady, putting her hand to her mouth in surprise. Looking down at Lucy, the housekeeper realized the little girl was lying on a body. "Bless my soul," she gasped.

"What is going on out here?" shouted Lucy's father appearing in the kitchen doorway. He hustled over to the pair, lantern in hand. Lucy knew she was in trouble when she heard his voice. It wasn't the first time she had been in the middle of a strange situation that wasn't appropriate for a Bishop's daughter to be involved in. Trouble just seemed to find her. She was sure, however, that it wasn't her fault this time. She needed to set the story straight before her father jumped to any unpleasant conclusions.

"Papa, he's a Palace guard," Lucy began to explain. She wanted to tell him how brave the young man had been and that she'd witnessed his attempt to stop an intruder. But she was shaking from the cold and was afraid she'd bite off her tongue with her chattering teeth if she tried to continue.

Luckily at that moment, the guard stirred and let out a moan of pain sparing Lucy from having to speak further. Lucy felt both grateful and relieved that the guard was still alive. She wouldn't have to explain why she was outside in the middle of the night in a dirty nightgown with a dead body anymore.

"Get Lucy into the vicarage, woman," Lucy's father commanded after taking in the situation. "It seems that this fellow needs some help. And wake up the Vicar."

Two

Building a Mission

Pacific Ocean, *two months later*

Thousands of miles across the seas a ship was headed for the Sandwich Islands.

Lucy had all but forgotten the night before they set sail, the night that she saved a Palace guard's life. She'd been at sea for two months now, and her journey was finally coming to an end.

She hadn't exactly enjoyed the voyage, in fact, she hated being cooped up in the vessel the whole time. Every day at sea, white sails flapped in the wind and a feisty crew of sailors went about their chores without any notice of the little eight year old girl hidden away in her quarters below deck.

If it weren't for her books and insect collection to keep her mind occupied, Lucy would have been scared. She'd overheard horrific stories of pirates from other missionary families who came to visit her town in the Cotswold that would make a person's hair stand on end. She loved to read, so she would escape into a story's adventure to keep her fears and imagination under control.

Lucy was all alone now. She and her father were taking the trip across the seas together but he hardly kept her company and it saddened her that her mother was no longer with them. It had been less than a year since she'd died. Lucy missed all the stories they had shared. *Mum*, she thought to herself, *you would have loved this new adventure, and I wish you were here.*

Lucy also missed her school friends. She didn't know what school would be like on the small island. She tried not to worry about it, and comforted herself with the knowledge that she still had her insect friends.

Suddenly she glanced at something tiny run across the floor with great speed. Lucy dropped to her knees and peered into the shadows under the furniture. "Gotcha!" she exclaimed, reaching out quickly with her arm. She felt the insect squirm under her small cupped hand. "Really? Miss Lady!"

Rows of meticulously labeled glass jars lined the shelf next to her trunk. They were covered with paper lids and were the homes to the various insects Lucy had gathered in England.

She wanted to be a scientist someday, and she planned to publish a book on insects when she was older. The beetles were Lucy's favorite because they reminded her of the fat old ladies in the village back home with their round rumps. She knew her father had no interest at all in the insects that shared their space on the ship so it was up to her to keep them safely tucked away in her corner in order for them to survive.

"Now, where is that home of yours?" Lucy asked out loud.

It was in just that moment she saw the container labeled *Lady Bug* roll past her feet with the rocking of the ship. She sucked in a breath when she realized that the jar was headed for a crash.

Lucy quickly dove forward on her belly, careful not to squish Miss Lady, and grabbed the jar just before it smashed. She let out a sigh of relief before carefully getting up with the two delicate things in her hands.

"I don't know what I'm going to do with you! This is your second escape in two days!"

Lucy examined the paper lid and noticed a small puncture. Ripping off a small cloth piece from her hemline, she stuffed it into the hole. "That ought to hold you!" she boasted triumphantly, securing Miss Lady back into her jar.

Every evening at about sunset, Lucy's father met with his assistant and foreman on the upper deck of the ship.

"Listen up guvnor, I don't want interfering from you or anyone else," said the foreman with a determined tone. He had job to do, and felt if it took brute force to turn the islanders into good workers, then so be it.

"It's got to be done with some measure of delicacy, I tell you," argued the Bishop.

"And I'm only saying that it was all handled poorly before. The islanders don't need understanding. A good firm English hand will do just fine," continued the foreman.

"We hired you to get the mission built in six months. So, we expect you to do it right – without physically coercing the islanders. We want results," replied the Bishop.

"And you'll get them," the foreman assured the Bishop. His name was Burles, and he had a nasty habit of smoking a cigar in the evening. He leaned on the railing and looked out at the horizon. The sun was dipping into the ocean but storm clouds brewed in the distance. He furrowed his brows wondering if he had time to smoke his cigar before the rains came down. He had a lot to think about because he was not prepared for the Bishop to have a strong character. The clergyman wouldn't be so easy to manipulate as Burles had planned.

Below deck Lucy sat with a book on her bed. But she couldn't focus on the story. She was worried about her father and his preoccupation with getting to the island quickly to begin his mission. He seemed on edge, restless with worry. Perhaps he was scared. After all, there were the stories of pirates at sea. Maybe her father needed someone to protect them and that would explain why he'd brought a young Scottish cleric with them on the voyage. Reverend Machesney had untamed red hair and a huge towering stature. He was an ambitious man assigned to assist Lucy's father at the new mission. All the same, Lucy didn't like her father's assistant and was glad that the young Reverend pretty much ignored her.

Most every day at sunset, her father and his assistant stood on the ship's deck reviewing the plans for the new mission settlement while Lucy remained in her cabin. There were dangers at sea. Many missionaries who had come before them perished at sea when the storms crushed their ships, while others were killed by pirates. But danger didn't keep Lucy's father from making the journey to meet the island's Chief. He felt a strong sense of duty to teach him and his people about God, the true God, and was sure he would be successful where others were not.

But he wouldn't be the first missionary to settle on the island of Maui. The McBeal family had arrived many years before, and started a school. There were thousands of islanders and the McBeals could no longer run the mission school by themselves and had asked the Diocese to send help.

Lucy's father had bigger plans beyond that. He dreamed of an entire mission town full of stores, schools that would teach everyone to read English, a church, and a printing company to print books. The Bishop hired Burles to build his vision for him while he focused on converting the islanders. Burles had been all too ready to leave England and begin a new life somewhere else when the Bishop met him in London. Both men instantly seized the opportunity they saw in the other. Now they just had to hammer out the details.

Meanwhile, Lucy was below deck. She could feel the chill of the night fill the cabin again as it snuck through the gap under the door and she was thankful that there were only a few more nights of this voyage at sea.

She couldn't wait to go to sleep in a real bed in a real room again. Although the cottage the family owned in the Cotswold was small, it was home, where she'd been able to curl up in front of the fireplace and warm her feet. The cabin on the ship was nothing more than a large closet with a musty smell seeping out of the boards which made her nauseous.

She quickly pulled off her wrinkled, green plaid dress, fold it, and placed it atop her books in the steamer trunk.

Three

The Cigar Smoking Man

The white porcelain wash basin in her cabin was empty. And there weren't any bathrooms on the ship or any running water.

"Blasts, why me every time?" she complained, looking into the dry basin. She wanted to wash her face before bed, but now she had to grab the bucket and go fetch the water first.

Lucy opened the wooden cabin door and took a cautious step through the arch into the long, dark corridor. She heard the crew laughing and singing beyond the shadowed abyss that awaited her.

The water barrel was chained to a beam at the other end of the corridor. Lucy slowly sucked in a breath of air to steady herself, but her throat seemed to tighten as she inhaled.

"Courage, young lady," she whispered to herself as her eyes tried to adjust to see down the hall, barely lit by the faint light filtering through the upper deck's floor grate.

The thunder in the night sky had stopped, but the crashing waves still pounded against the hull of the ship, making it rock back and forth violently. It was a scary place to be. There was no telling who Lucy would meet outside her cabin, maybe a drunken sailor or another passenger lurking in the shadows – both very frightening to a small girl by herself in the dark.

She really disliked filling the bucket. And at night it was worse because the odor of moldy rags and musty straw lingering in the air got stronger. She pinched her nose to keep from gagging on the disgusting smell and pressed on, gliding her fingers along the wall and counting each cabin door along the way. "Eight, seven, six, five," she whispered to herself.

She was about to count the fourth when the quiet of the corridor was interrupted by voices coming from the steps near her cabin. She turned to see who it was but couldn't make out the figures. As they continued talking in hushed words, she recognized her father and Reverend Machesney's voices. She stood very still, holding the empty bucket close to her body while watching the men go into their respective cabins.

Lucy let out the breath she didn't know she was holding in, just as another man descended the stairs. *He is huge*, thought Lucy as she slowly scooted back towards the water barrel. She could only see his silhouette in the darkness but the lingering odor of a cigar drifted down in the corridor as he approached.

She began to tremble and her knuckles went white from clinging to the sides of the barrel. But she didn't dare move another muscle with the stranger's footsteps coming closer. For a moment she closed her eyes and pretended that she was invisible, which was silly because she was not more than five feet from the man now, but she pretended all the same. And to her amazement, when she opened her eyes she saw that he had vanished. She hoped he had gone into his cabin.

Lucy, not eager to encounter any more passengers, dunked the bucket into the barrel and was side-stepping a puddle when she noticed a shiny object on the floor. A brilliant gold shined in a beam of moonlight now coming through the grate above. Lucy reached down and was about to pick up the coin she found just as a large wave smacked against the side of the ship and the bucket fell, spilling her water and making the floor slippery. Knocked off balance by the powerful jolt, she frantically grabbed for the closest thing to steady herself; it was the door knob to Cabin One.

Lucy's fingers grasped the cold metal, but she quickly let go when she felt her feet slide out from under her and then she plopped straight down on her bum against the cabin door.

"Ouch!" she cried out. Recovering quickly, she leaned forward and grabbed the gold coin off the floor and picked up the water bucket.

The door to Cabin One swung open and an enormous body filled the doorway. "What the blazes!" growled the cigar-smoking man.

Lucy looked up into the face of the giant, but all she could make out in the shadows was his round head and the red glow of his cigar. He looked like a demon and it frightened her. She quickly straightened herself up, tucking her hands under her legs to conceal the coin. She clenched the object so tightly the sharp edge dug into her skin.

"Aren't you the Bishop's kid?" he asked, grabbing Lucy up by her arm.

"Let me go," she demanded, wiggling to be set free and holding her hand with the coin behind her back.

"Hum," he replied. "Hiding something?" He reached for her hand and smiled as he easily pulled it forward.

Lucy was determined not to give up the coin without a struggle and tried to make it impossible for the man to pry the coin out of her hand. But all the squirming didn't deter him from opening each of her delicate fingers one at a time, like peeling away a banana's skin.

"And what do we have here?" he said mockingly. "Didn't your father teach you not to take what doesn't belong to you?"

"I found it!" Lucy exclaimed just before Burles snatched her up by both arms. She was afraid that he was going to shake the living daylights out of her.

"Ouch! You're hurting me! Let go!" Lucy screamed, kicking at him with her dangling legs. The cigar-smoking man merely held her farther away and squeezed her arms harder. Lucy closed her eyes against the pain and made a desperate wish. She thought then that if God granted prayers, this was as good a time as any to ask Him for a favor.

Whoosh! Lucy felt a blast of wind come out of nowhere and swirl through her hair. The sides of the ship creaked and groaned under a mighty gale. She watched the man struggle to keep his footing as the gust got stronger, and before Lucy realized it, the two of them were being hurled across the corridor.

Lucy wasted no time in escaping. She grabbed the bucket and scrambled on her hands and knees all the way back to Cabin Eight. She didn't dare look back.

Four

Maui – June, 1826

Lucy couldn't stop hopping up and down with excitement. "Miss Lady," she said to her constant companion, "you won't believe your eyes. Well, of course you will when you see it, but it is fantastic!"

Lucy awoke in the early morning hours to silver ribbons shimmering across the surface of a soft blue blanket of water. She had to blink and rub her eyes when she first peeked at the sea from the cabin's porthole. Then she saw that they had landed at the base of a gigantic mountain which soared high into the heavens.

Still hopping up and down, she struggled to pull on her dress and button up her shoes. During the entire voyage Lucy feared that she would drown. Now that they had landed in the Sandwich Islands, she was not only relieved her worry was behind her, but also extremely eager to feel solid ground beneath her feet.

Without a warning, the cabin door flew open.

"Well, we're here!" announced her father cheerily still trying to catch his breath from the excitement.

Lucy laughed at the sight of him. His eyes looked like they were going to pop right out of his head with delight. She hadn't seen him this happy in almost a year.

"Good, you're already dress," he remarked, quickly scanning the room. "Now all this silliness of hiding down here below deck can come to an end." He grabbed her hand and they left the cabin heading up the stairs.

"Where are the houses, Papa?" asked Lucy as they came up on deck and she looked at the island again.

"Oh, there will be houses soon enough. You can be sure of that," her father replied enthusiastically.

"Move it, you two," ordered the Captain, pushing them to the ship's rail. He turned to his crew and yelled, "Anchors down?"

"Aye, aye captain!" replied the crew.

"Sails all tight?" he asked.

"Aye, aye, all tight!" chorused the sailors.

"Get a move on, lads. Lower the boats."

The sandy shoreline was not too far off in the distance when Lucy was lowered into a small boat. Surrounded by numerous other boats, the sailor manning Lucy's boat rowed slowly toward land. There really was no reason to hurry with the water so crowded. The sun was shining and the calmness of the sea was welcoming too. But Lucy was restless. She couldn't wait to get to the island.

"Hold still," commanded her father. But his words couldn't calm her fidgeting.

She felt like she was in a dream. Before her eyes hundreds of women were swimming towards them. They looked like mermaids with their long black hair trailing behind on the waters' surface. And standing on the beach was an army of chocolate colored men. Yes, she knew she must be dreaming.

As they got closer, Lucy couldn't help but notice two young boys at the dock. She realized that they couldn't be islanders because they had light skin and dressed in formal British clothes. *Good,* she thought, *I will have some playmates.* She noticed that one was tall with dark hair, and the other was short with curly blonde hair that looked like a frizzy mop framing his round face.

Back on the shore the boys were puzzled by what they saw too. "Suppose it's them?" asked the taller boy.

"Aye, must be!" replied the one with the mop on his head.

"What's she doin' now?" asked the taller boy.

"I thought they were bringin' a lad," said the younger boy, feeling let down. "She's got blonde curls. This isn't goin' ter be any fun at all!"

"Blimey, she's runnin'!"

The two boys stood with their hands in their pockets and watched Lucy sprint down the dock in a matter of seconds, pass them, and plant her shoes in the golden sand. They slowly followed her to the beach, the taller boy raising an eyebrow as he passed Lucy and walked away.

"Excuse me," asked the younger boy, "with the Bishop Tuppins' party, are yeh?"

"Yes, I'm Lucy Tuppins," she replied, bending down to pick up a few shells poking out of the sand.

"Oh, we were expectin' a laddie, that's all," he continued, reaching into his pocket and pulling out a huge frog. The boy immediately thrust it towards Lucy's face in hopes of shocking her.

"Why, thank you!" she exclaimed, taking the creature from him.

The younger boy's face filled with disappointment. Not only was she not a boy, but she didn't scare easily like most girls.

"Yeh're not scared?" he asked perplexed, curling his lower lip outward.

"Of a little frog? No!" she laughed.

"Got warts, he has."

"He's fantastic! Thank you." Lucy beamed at the boy. Then she noticed that the taller boy was standing at the edge of the forest. He was holding the reins of a horse attached to a buggy. "Who's that?" she asked.

"'Tis my brother, Eugene."

"Does he always dress like that?" she remarked.

"Aye. I guess he – I mean, we thought yeh might be a – yeh're a girl!" He stumbled over his words when he looked at Lucy and blushed slightly.

She was quite amused and flattered too; so she twirled around once and then curtsied, her skirt rippling in the warm tropical breeze.

"Well, I'm sorry to have ruined your expectations."

The boy smiled and shook his head. "Yeh bein' a lassie, that's okay by me. Name's Oliver," he said, extending his hand. Lucy shook it warmly and then Oliver led Lucy up to the edge of the forest to introduce her to his brother.

Eugene, the older one, acted mature beyond his years and dressed like a miniature missionary. He took great pride in polishing his shiny boots every morning and made sure he had excellent posture at all times. He greeted Lucy with a stare that made her skin crawl.

"Look Eugene, she's not all that bad. She likes my frog!" said Oliver.

Not a word came out of the older boy. He just kept staring at her with disapproval. Lucy felt humiliated. She thought that he should show some manners by at least saying hello. All he did was tug at the ends of his vest while encircling her. She asked herself, *what does he think he's doing? After all, I'm not a horse waiting for inspection.*

"I'm as good a climber and runner as any boy," she announced defensively.

"I doubt that. Yeh won' last a day out here in those frilly thin's," he scoffed, touching her pinafore.

"Let's take Lucy ter the cave tomorrow, Eugene," Oliver suggested, trying to stop his brother from ruining his chances of making a new friend, even if she was only a girl and not the laddie he had hoped for.

"Oh sure. She'll be ballin' her little head off before we cross the stream. No thanks," Eugene replied.

Lucy let out an exasperated huff. "I will not!"

"Besides, the bugs will eat yeh alive with all that smelly stuff yeh're wearin'," Eugene said, leaning into sniff at her shoulder.

Lucy could hear the disdain dripping from his words and she was fed up with his rudeness. She dodged sideways just as he bent down, and laughter rolled out of Oliver at the sight of his brother falling flat on his face.

Oliver, still with a huge grin on his face, wrapped his arm around Lucy and started escorting her back down to the dock to avoid his brother's wrath.

Lucy turned to look back over her shoulder and gave Eugene a bit of advice, "I'd be careful if I were you. Don't be so quick to judge people you don't know."

Eugene knew then from that time onward he would have to be one step ahead of this girl if he was going to put her in her place.

At the end of the dock, Lucy and Oliver greeted her father.

"And who do we have here?" the Bishop asked Lucy.

"Papa, this is Oliver."

"Hello, young man," he greeted the mop-haired boy.

"They've come to fetch us in the buggy," Lucy continued, pointing out Eugene standing with his arms folded across his chest, his lips pouted in disgust.

"That's my brother, Eugene. We're supposed ter give yeh a proper welcome on the shore," Oliver explained.

"Well then, what are we waiting for?" the Bishop asked. "Lucy, your basket of bugs is on the end of the dock."

"You left them there? You've probably killed them, Papa!" She rushed over to the basket and lifted the rag covering the jars, letting out a sigh of relief when she saw that they were all safe.

Five

A New Friend

It may have been the fact that everyone around her was having a good time, singing as they hustled with the cargo on the shoreline. *Such wonderment to be found in this magical place,* thought Lucy.

Oliver, Lucy, and the Bishop made their way up the beach toward the buggy and joined Eugene.

"'Tis with great pleasure, sir, that the McBeal family welcomes yeh ter Maui," he announced with the click of his boot heels and a bow. "We've come ter fetch yeh in our buggy."

If first impressions were important, then Eugene must have just scored a lot of points with my father, thought Lucy. But Eugene wasn't fooling her and she had already realized that his cold stare was nothing to fear. She was going to enjoy changing his mind about girls.

"I expected to meet your father," said the Bishop, looking around for an adult. "It's been such a long journey."

"We've waited fer some time now fer yehr arrival," the young brother explained, readjusting his glasses on the bridge of his pudgy nose. "We've been comin' down here every mornin' fer days ter greet yeh."

"Surely, you're not here by yourselves among all these islanders!" Lucy asked with alarm in her voice.

"Known them fer two years now, nothin' ter be afraid of," Eugene boasted.

"Besides, they all go ter our mam's school," followed up Oliver.

Lucy watched the boys with curiosity. She estimated Eugene to be about eleven years old, which made him three years older than she was. She had to hold her laughter back when he spoke in his serious Scottish brogue. *Maybe he has possibilities,* she thought. His neatly-groomed dark curly hair made him attractive, but his gangly-thin legs would keep him from ever being a serious athlete, and she was quite certain she could outrun him any day.

As for the younger brother, Oliver, he was more to her liking. She thought he was probably nine years old. That made him only one year older than she was. He obviously was not very mature since he carried a frog in his pocket all day. Lucy admired Oliver's audacity in attempting to frighten her with it. His short stocky legs and unkempt blonde hair made her think that they were better-suited to be playmates. She sensed that he enjoyed climbing and getting dirty just as much as she did. She decided this boy who wore a brown shirt and knickers comfortably was definitely her favorite.

"Come on, then," said Oliver getting into the buggy. "Our father is just ahead in the village, through the jungle. The trip won' take long."

Lucy listened to Eugene offer bits of information as he drove them through the jungle.

"The islanders call that mountain, *Haleakala,* or House of the Sun," explained Eugene, pointing up through the trees, "and was once a volcano, spewin' lava everywhere."

But Lucy and her father couldn't concentrate on the tour because they were getting tired and very uncomfortable in the hot humid temperatures. Sweat dripped off the Bishop's brow, and Lucy tugged at her moist, sticky clothing. She realized then why the islanders wore little material to cover their bodies. It was just too hot for proper British clothing.

She sat back and watched the vines draping across the forest canopy. The aroma of ginger and the sweet white *pikake* flower was so woody and calming. While Eugene's voice droned on, she found her eyelids closing for the rest of the trip. When the buggy came to a halt, she opened her eyes.

"Everyone out," instructed Eugene.

"Why?" asked Lucy.

She hadn't noticed yet that they were out of the forest already and at the end of a road located at the base of a gigantic mountain. It looked like a colossal staircase to Lucy, with layers of green velvet terraces ascending up the side of the hill.

"Just a short walk from here," said Oliver, helping Lucy from the buggy.

Lucy had a headache. As she approached a gathering, she heard the pounding and singing of ancient island cadences and the sounds were making her headache worse. She covered her ears and looked up. Lucy's eyes settled on a cluster of heads peering out over a high stone wall near the top of the mountain. Their fierce teeth and bulging eyes made her stop in her tracks and forget about the headache.

"Oliver, look!" she exclaimed, pointing at the grotesque heads.

"Oh," he said, looking at the heads above. "They're just made out of wood. Nothin' ter fear."

"They sure look real to me," she said, eyeing them skeptically. "Are you sure they aren't warriors?"

"Aye, I'm sure," he replied pushing her further into the crowd.

She was greeted by the sight of thousands of islanders gathered on the lower terrace, singing their rhythms louder and louder. A shrill voice suddenly rose above the crowd, out of place in the islanders' symphony of sounds.

"It's Mam!" shouted Oliver, seeing Lucy's alarm.

Mrs. McBeal nudged her way through the bodies like a fine silver knife slicing a pound of butter with one hand while lifting the hem of her long black linen dress, and with her strong commanding Scottish tone called out "Bishop Tuppins! Bishop Tuppins!" while waving to them with her free hand.

Lucy laughed when she saw a short man stumbling along in the Scottish woman's wake. It was undoubtedly the Reverend McBeal, and Lucy thought that he resembled Oliver with his hair bobbing back and forth like a gray cloud of fuzzy mist.

"I see my boys have given yeh a proper welcome," puffed the Reverend when he reached the new arrivals.

"Yes, they are smart chaps. And it's good to see you again, Reverend McBeal," the Bishop said, greeting him with a hand shake.

"Aloha," said Mrs. McBeal, curtsying before Lucy. "Welcome to Maui."

Instead of properly returning Mrs. McBeal's greeting, Lucy said the first thing that popped into her head. "What kind of insects do you have?"

"Lucy! Mind your manners," scolded her father, looking downward in a stern scowl.

"I'm sorry, Papa," she quickly apologized. Lucy turned to Mrs. McBeal again, this time with a curtsy and a smile. "It's a pleasure to meet you too." She didn't know what had gotten into her, except that she was probably overwhelmed with everything around her.

Then she heard the resonating dry foghorn sound vibrating against the mountain sides and tree tops.

Six

Chief Ke'eaumoku

High above their heads on the mountain was a boy. He stood tall, with both hands around a huge conch shell pressed to his lips. As he blew air into the shell, the islanders stood and became silently motionless. No one dared speak or move.

When the boy stopped sounding the conch, Lucy watched the islanders split into two groups, leaving a gaping path as wide as a cathedral aisle in front of the Bishop. It reminded her of the story of Moses parting the Red Sea. But instead of the sea it was people this time. She waited anxiously to see what was going to happen next.

Before the crowd stood the biggest man Lucy had ever seen. He towered over everyone measuring seven feet tall. She watched him raise a large staff and the islanders slowly knelt down on the yellowed grass. Lucy figured that for this big man to command all these people to kneel, he must be the Chief.

Lucy felt Mrs. McBeal's hand around her wrist and before she knew it they were making their way to the front and center in front of the Chief. *I wonder why he isn't wearing a crown,* thought Lucy. She looked upward at the sleek dark skinned man draped in a long cape made of yellow and red feathers. She leaned over to Oliver and said, "My, what a giant he is!"

"Shush!" Oliver replied. "He's the *Ali'i* – royalty."

"But – "

"Lucy!" he grabbed her hand with a jerk. "Yeh're goin' ter cause trouble, shush!"

"I am Governor Ke'eaumoku, brother to Queen Ka'ahumanu and Kaheiheimaile," the Chief announced, thumping his staff on the ground twice. His deep voice rumbled throughout the valley.

Reverend McBeal was the first one to respond, pulling the Bishop by the sleeve and hurrying him toward the platform.

Lucy didn't want to be left behind, so she kept in step behind the two clergymen.

"Chief," said Reverend McBeal, "Let me present Bishop Tuppins."

"Delighted to be invited to your island, your honor," recited the Bishop, bowing as low as his head could go. He felt intimidated by the mere size of the ruler, and sincerely hoped that he would never lose his head over any future misunderstandings with the Chief.

"And what news you bring from across the great water?" asked the Chief.

Why does he want to know about stuff going on in England?, thought Lucy. She watched her father stumble over his words and he finally replied, "News?"

Seeing the helpless look on the Bishop's face, Reverend McBeal seized upon a more specific topic. "Tell him anything... tell him about the Queen."

Lucy's father turned back toward the Chief and cleared his throat as if he was about to deliver an important sermon. "Well, your honor," he began, "most recently the Queen of England was robbed."

No one was more surprised at that comment then Lucy herself. She couldn't help giggle at the bewildered look on Reverend McBeal's face.

"Blimey, sir!" The Reverend whispered fiercely to the Bishop. "What are yeh thinkin'? Better not be tellin' this one any untruths."

"Oh, but it is true!" assured the Bishop before continuing. "The day we set sail it was in all the newspapers."

"Ah," said the Chief, nodding in approval. "I hear that your Queen is a powerful woman. Owns plenty land."

The Bishop blinked a couple of times in puzzlement at the Chief's comment. "Well, yes, that it true. She is the most powerful woman in the British Empire."

"Reverend has told us much about your country. Later, you and I will talk." The Chief nodded again.

Lucy had been listening attentively, but when a little yellow finch landed on the Chief's cape and began burrowing under the feathers, she started to laugh.

"I want to learn more about your Queen," the ruler continued to speak, but stopped when he heard Lucy and raised his staff to point it within inches of her chest. "Come here little *keiki*," he commanded with a frown.

Lucy gasped and clasped both of her hands over her mouth. *Now I've gone and done it. I'm in real big trouble. Probably the worst trouble in my whole life,* she thought to herself. She hoped that these people didn't make human sacrifices. She'd lose her head by nightfall for sure. Thinking quickly, she took a few large deliberate steps forward to stand in front of the Chief and curtsied.

"Terribly sorry, sir," she squeaked in a faint voice.

She could feel the man's warm breath as he leaned forward, hovering just over her head. Lucy was terrified. *Oh, this is definitely the worst day of my life!* She thought. Lucy could barely look up at the Chief. But when she finally did, she diverted his attention with her hand. All eyes followed where she pointed, fixed on a small bird peeking out from under the Chief's cape.

The great man looked back at Lucy and stared with his big brown eyes. He touched her blonde curls, ruffling them with his long fingers. Her knees began to shake and she thought she would faint right then and there.

Suddenly, the Chief smiled.

"You are the *keiki* in my dreams. With hair that shines like the sun. A sign of good things for my people," he said to Lucy before raising up and shouting this in his own language. The islanders cheered at this announcement.

Lucy had a bad habit of speaking before thinking about what she was going to say. Most times it got her into a lot of trouble. And that is exactly what happened next.

"How could I be in your dreams? I'm from England!" she protested in a quiet voice. But the ruler still heard her.

"I said you are! I am the Chief, *Ali'i*, brother to Queen Ka'ahumanu and Queen Kaheiheimaile," he replied with finality.

"But, your honor, I –", she started to argue, but the Chief bent down with a scowl that scared her half to death.

Before she recovered her wits enough to try again, the ruler pounded the dirt with his staff. Lucy felt the ground shake beneath her shoes because the staff was within inches of smashing her toes. The Chief was no longer interested in what Lucy had to say. It was then that Lucy felt the Reverend McBeal pull her by the waist and whisk her behind the Bishop. And just in time, too!

Everyone watched as the Chief left the platform, ending the audience. Then the islanders dispersed into the forest and to the fishing villages.

"The Chief likes yeh, Lucy," warned Eugene, "but yeh better learn somethin' now. When it comes ter the Chief, all yeh're supposed ter do is listen. Yeh'd better keep that mouth of yehrs shut."

"Well, Eugene," huffed Lucy, placing her hands on her hips. "You could have told me before now! As for my mouth, it has a habit of expressing itself without my control sometimes."

"Yeh should pray about that," the older boy replied, teasingly.

"Now, now," said the Bishop, seeing that his daughter and the boy were not on good terms.

"The Queen! Is it true?" asked Oliver.

"Yes, it happened the day before we left England," confirmed the Bishop.

"It was a mysterious criminal," piped up Lucy. "He stole the Queen's money."

"Blimey!" exclaimed Oliver.

"And now our Queen's poor," she added in a serious tone. "Scrubbing floors, can you imagine?"

"Lucy Tuppins!" scolded the Bishop. "Enough tales."

"Well, she lost her money, didn't she?" the little girl said defensively. But her father ignored her instead, turning to his host.

"Been two months since then, surely the thieves have been captured?" asked the Reverend.

Lucy felt Oliver's hand grab at her arm and pull her toward the buggy.

"Never mind all that, yeh'll be pleased with the house. A big climin' tree, it has," he told her.

"And soft beds," Lucy pondered happily, "and a real kitchen with smells of cinnamon and spices, too, I hope."

Seven

THE WHITE HOUSE

They were in the buggy and riding along the forest path again. But this time, they were headed for a small village where the McBeals had built a mission school.

Lucy leaned out the side of the buggy trying to get a better look at the trees and flowers when a large leaf the size of an elephant's ear swiped the side of the cart and hit her in the head.

Oliver quickly reached over and yanked her back into the buggy before she fell out.

"Yeh did that on purpose," he accused Eugene.

"She shouldn' be hangin' over the edge," the older brother replied with a snort.

"I'm alright, Oliver," reassured Lucy. She straightened the hem of her dress and sat closer to him on the bench.

"Haven't yeh seen big leaves before?" asked Oliver.

"Of course I have! But not like these."

As they continued, Lucy marveled at the long *maile* vines weaving like gigantic spider webs through the branches above. Her head twisted right and left as they passed foliage in vibrant hues of yellow, green, red, orange, and purple. She didn't' know if she could ever accurately describe this incredible forest to anyone. It was as if she was dreaming of a fantasy island.

Although the ride seemed to take hours, the thought of exploring this new world occupied Lucy's mind. Her imagination conjured up thrilling adventures with jungle creatures and secret hiding places. She wished that Eugene would drive the buggy even slower, but they were part of a caravan of carts and wagons taking supplies into the village and probably had to remain with the group.

"Hey, look at this one," said Oliver, leaning over the side to snatch a passing *haupu* fern.

Just then, one of the carts came up quickly from behind and Eugene grabbed Oliver by his belt, giving a swift tug to reel his brother back inside the buggy before colliding with the other driver. "Honestly, Oliver," he complained, "yeh'll get yerself decapitated if yeh don' watch it."

"Aw! Yeh're no fun," whined Oliver.

"How can you boys bicker at a time like this!" remarked Lucy, still absorbing the surroundings. "Just look at how amazing this place is. That tree over there almost looks like a giant, ready to pounce down at any moment, and whoosh! Swoop up an intruder."

Before long they were riding through a tunnel. Everything around them went dark.

"Oooooooooh! Watch out!" joked Oliver. "*Menehune* hide out in these tunnels."

"Good Lord, Oliver!" exclaimed Eugene, embarrassed for his brother. "Don' mind him, he's got feathers fer brains."

"*Menehunes*. What are those?" asked Lucy.

"Little people," Oliver explained. "Ah, magic they are."

"Teller of tales, this one," said Eugene, rolling his eyes.

Suddenly, a rock dislodged from the moist wall and fell to the ground next to the buggy, startling Lucy. She slid so close to Oliver on the seat that she sat on his pant leg. She loved a good story, but Oliver's tale just might have some truth in it.

"Listen, she's not goin' ter fall fer it. Don' waste yehr breath," advised Eugene.

"Quiet, Eugene," snapped Lucy, turning to Oliver. "Do their eyes glow in the dark?"

"Great! Now there are two of yeh!" sighed Eugene.

"Eugene's never seen one, have yeh then!" teased Oliver as he leaned forward onto his brother's shoulder.

Sitting upright, Eugene folded his arms across his chest. "Oh, and I suppose yeh have?"

"Aye, I have," replied Oliver. "They're awfully helpful if yer're lost, they'll get yeh home fer sure."

Just then, the buggy exited the tunnel and entered a clearing. A tall gangly border of trees lined the road up ahead.

"There. See?" announced Eugene. "Safe and sound, and without any *Menehune* I might add."

As they rounded a bend in the road, Lucy noticed a building. "Wow!" she marveled, gazing at a house nestled in a field of tall flowing grasses. And it wasn't just any house, but the most beautiful two-story home she'd ever seen. It glimmered invitingly in the afternoon sun, with white boards that looked freshly painted. She wondered if the porch wrapped around the entire first floor, and how many bedrooms it housed.

"Aye, and I told yeh there was a climbin' tree," reminded Oliver, pointing ahead.

Lucy somehow managed to wait the rest of the way with extreme restraint before jumping out of the buggy.

"Where are yeh goin?" Oliver cried out.

"I don't wait!" she yelled, running through the reeds of grass towards her new home and her father who had arrived first.

The front door of the white clapboard house opened. Lucy saw a beautiful slender girl stroll out onto the porch. Her delicate white skirt billowed in the wind like a sail.

"Hello!" she called, waving to the arrivals.

The yard was full of carts being unloaded of fresh food stuffs while the McBeals and Tuppins disembarked their buggies.

"Papa," Lucy said, catching up with her father and tightly hugging him. "Isn't it fantastic?"

"Yes, it is," he replied with a rare smile.

Everyone gathered on the porch and Mrs. McBeal started the introductions. "Bishop," she said, "I'd like fer yeh ter meet my daughter, Elizabeth."

Lucy was curious. She hadn't considered that Eugene and Oliver might have an older sister. It was also obvious to her that her father thought Elizabeth as attractive.

"It's a pleasure," he said, bowing before her.

"We are glad that yeh've come ter join us, Bishop Tuppins," Elizabeth replied with a blush before turning to Lucy. "And what a pleasure ter meet such a fine young lady," she addressed the young girl while curtsying.

Lucy smiled warmly and curtsied back.

The Revered Machesney grew restless. He was getting annoyed that his turn at introductions hadn't come yet and was impatient to meet Elizabeth, too. He cleared his throat in a rather disgusting manner to get everyone's attention. They all turned to look at him.

"Oh! Well then," said Bishop Tuppins, remembering his manners and breaking himself away from the loveliness of Elizabeth. "Let me introduce my assistant, Reverend Machesney."

Lucy knew the formalities had to be done before she could really have any fun, so she stood patiently while everyone finished saying hello. But Reverend Machesney did something that was just not done by a clergyman – he kissed Elizabeth's hand! Lucy gasped. *How rude of him! Elizabeth was obviously a respectable girl.* Lucy was mortified at the thought that his actions would reflect badly on her and her father. Poor manners were just poor manners and she wanted no part of his impropriety.

"What a pleasure ter meet such a fine young lass," he declared, holding her hand in his. His eyes fixed on Elizabeth with a hungry stare he continued, "And out here in the jungle, too."

Elizabeth was too polite to point out the breach so she ignored it. She slowly retrieved her hand from the young clergyman's persistent grasp, then turned to Lucy.

"I understand yeh're a very good student," she commented to Lucy.

"Yes, mam," agreed Lucy.

"Then we are goin' ter get along just fine," said Elizabeth. "Yeh see, I'm yehr teacher and we are goin' ter have some grand adventures while yeh are here. Now, let me show yeh to yehr bedroom."

Lucy grinned. She was delighted to meet Elizabeth, and was confident that her new teacher was a strong woman who could handle the likes of Reverend Machesney.

Eight

Bugs and Things

Lucy's little purse hung from the bedpost in her room. She still couldn't believe that she had a room of her own. Just outside her bedroom door was a balcony overlooking the house's grand staircase.

A large wooden wardrobe made of the swirling red and brown grains of *koa* wood rested against the wall across from Lucy's four poster bed. Elizabeth was hanging the girl's dresses in the wardrobe when there was a knock at the door.

"Hi Oliver, come on in," said Elizabeth.

He entered carrying a basket. "I don' know what's so important about a bunch of jars, but here it is," he said, putting it on the floor beside the bed.

"Hey, be careful with that," demanded Lucy, rising from the soft mattress. "Do you want to see? This one is my favorite." She picked out a jar from the basket and un-wrapped the paper lid. "She's Miss Lady."

"Blimey, it's a bug with black spots!" he blurted. Oliver looked down into the basket with a lot more interest now that he realized it was full of bugs.

"Don' let our mam catch yeh with those up here," warned Elizabeth.

"She hates bugs," added Oliver, wrinkling up his nose.

"They're insects, Oliver," Lucy corrected him. "Not bugs."

"Alright, insects. They look all the same ter me," he conceded.

Lucy busied herself arranging each of her jars on the desk beside her bed. She'd only lost three insects during the voyage and was proud of herself for taking good care of her specimen collection.

Elizabeth took her brother by the shoulders and turned him toward the doorway. "Off with yeh now," she ordered. "Lucy and I have lots ter talk about – girl stuff."

Then Elizabeth pushed open the large window that over-looked the dirt road to one of the villages. She had been trained as a teacher in Scotland before moving with her parents to the island and loved living among the islanders. But she didn't have many friends because she was only sixteen and her parents did not allow her to mingle much with the local boys and girls.

"Yeh know, havin' another lassie around is goin' ter be grand," Elizabeth remarked. "I see yeh've labeled all yehr jars. Why?"

"It's my research," Lucy responded, sitting back on the bed next to Elizabeth.

"Research! Now what kind of research could yeh be doin'?"

"Insects. I'm going to be a scientist."

"Oh, yeh are?" Elizabeth asked with a smile.

"Yes."

"Well, that's an admirable quality, Miss Lucy. Confidence. I like that."

"Papa doesn't agree," confessed Lucy sadly. "He says that God made all the creatures on this earth, and that's enough for anyone to know. But I want to know a lot more. How they eat, when they sleep, and things like that."

"That's a good start, then. Say, would yeh like ter explore the forest and find more insects?" asked Elizabeth.

"Of course!" exclaimed Lucy, eyes brightening.

Elizabeth reached down and lifted a parcel off the floor. It was covered in a swatch of material and tied with a soft red ribbon. "This is from my mam. It's sort of a welcome present."

Lucy loved presents. She took great care in untying the ribbon. It reminded her of the last present she received. It was from her mother over a year ago, a silver locket.

The blue brown cloth that Lucy held up was scratchy and sewn into some sort of garment. But she didn't know if she was supposed to wear it, or why she would even want to. *What kind of present is this? Would I hurt Elizabeth's feelings if I said it was ugly?* Lucy thought again and decided that she'd better keep those thoughts in her head and just sit quietly on the bed.

"Well, do yeh like it?" asked Elizabeth.

"I don't know what it is?" she responded, trying to seem polite.

Elizabeth grabbed it and held it up to Lucy's shoulders, checking to see if the dimensions were proper. After all, her mam had to guess at the measurements of the eight year old. "She calls them travelin' clothes. There are not stores here, yeh know. She's made them fer all of us. But father doesn' know. He wouldn' approve that they show our knees. It's a secret."

Elizabeth helped Lucy pull off her dress and slipped the ugly one down over her head. There were two layers. Lucy wiggled and chafed from the scratchy material.

"It's not very comfortable," admitted Lucy.

"Oh," chuckled Elizabeth, "it's on backwards. Sorry. Mam worked all night sewin' it fer yeh."

"I'd rather wear those fabrics I saw the island girls wear around their hips," confided Lucy.

Elizabeth burst out in laughter. "As sure as the sun rises in the mornin', father would lock me up fer a year if he caught me in somethin' so skimpy. Don' imagine yehr father thinks any different."

Lucy stood up and walked over to the mirror in the wardrobe. *Not in a million years would I ever wear this out where anyone could see me,* she thought. "Elizabeth, I don't think I can wear this to church."

"Silly, it's not fer church. They're travelin' clothes. Fer the forest. Yeh did say that yeh wanted ter search fer insects, didn' yeh? Well, there yeh go, then," the older girl explained.

Lucy came back to the bed and removed the garment. It itched and she couldn't wait to get it off. "Why is it a secret?"

"Well, father has forbidden us ter go ter the waterfalls. But Oliver and Eugene just love ter swim in the cool water. Mam secretly made each of us a pair of clothes we could use ter get wet and dirty; that's all."

Lucy stuffed the garment back into the wrapper and handed it to Elizabeth. "Thanks, but I won't be needing this. I'm not going to a waterfall."

"Of course yeh are," insisted Elizabeth. "We have it all planned. Just imagine the cool drops of water flowing ever so gently, like a carpet of bubbles." She closed her eyes while her fingers rolled down in the air with the pretended drops of moisture. "Down, down, into a chilled pool."

Lucy nudged Elizabeth's shoulder. "Hot weather's gone and messed with your head. You've gone batty!" she teased.

"We're goin' tomorrow," announced Elizabeth.

Lucy felt fear rising in her gut. She couldn't stop the tear from pooling in her eyes. "Had enough water for a lifetime, thank you," she said, wiping her tears from her cheeks.

"Now yeh're just being silly. Have yeh ever even seen a waterfall?"

"I don't like water that moves," she mumbled, turning away from Elizabeth.

"It's okay. Don' cry," consoled Elizabeth, hugging her new friend for a minute. "Now tell me. Why don' yeh like the water?"

"I fell into the stream, near the Ebley Bridge by my home. It was awfully deep and choked me. I couldn't breathe."

"Did yehr father save you?" asked Elizabeth.

"No, it was Baron Gyde. There was a branch. My dress was all tangled up in it," continued Lucy, trying to hold back the tears. "And it was my best one, too."

"Oh. Then it was him that rescued yeh."

"Yes. You wouldn't believe how cold the water was. I couldn't feel my legs! Then when I finally opened my eyes, there he was, Baron Gyde and his sheep keeping me warm. He took me to his big house and wrapped me up in front of the fire."

"It sounds awfully frightenin'."

"It was," Lucy responded in a faraway voice. Then the little girl shuddered and took a deep breath declaring, "I'm never going in the water again. Ever!"

"Don' yeh worry, wee lassie, "said Elizabeth. "We won't let yeh be harmed. I promise." She stroked the little girl's cheek and gave her a smile of encouragement.

Elizabeth could tell now that Lucy was really exhausted from the trip. She remembered her own experience when she first made the journey to the Sandwich Islands and how over-whelming it had been. Her new little pupil probably needed a good night's rest just as she had back then. The little girl managed a weak smile and Elizabeth stood up, walking towards the door.

But as soon as she left, Lucy's mind flooded again with all the unpleasant memories. Trying to calm herself, she scooted out of bed and opened her steamer trunk to pull out a dried sprig of lavender. The familiar fragrance comforted Lucy and filled the room while she opened up her purse and pulled out her favorite trinkets – a pencil and a tiny notebook. She placed them on the desk in front of her jar collection.

Lucy knew that her life on the island was going to be very different. Thoughts of climbing new trees and exploring caves sounded fun. All she had to do is avoid the waterfalls.

Nine

KALANI

Morning arrived with the sounds of life bursting from the jungle. Lucy could hear the birds start singing the moment the sun peeked over the summit of *Haleakala*.

The white clapboard house was soon bustling with the McBeal and Tuppins families. There were chores to attend to but a good breakfast was most important first.

"As sure as the Good Lord has given us a fine day," stated Mrs. McBeal, pushing her way through the kitchen door, "we should be grateful fer such blessin's."

Lucy had been the first into the kitchen earlier in the morning and met Leah, the cook. But she would soon find out that it was Mrs. McBeal who planned all the meals, tended the garden, and kept the household flowing smoothly.

Everyone began taking seats on two long benches at a twelve-foot wooden table that took up most of the kitchen space. Mrs. McBeal, still pleasantly chatting in her commanding voice, plopped down on the other end of the bench Bishop Tuppins was on. He was half her weight, and before anyone realized what had happened, he was bounced up into the air and Mrs. McBeal was sitting on the floor. The laughter in the room was so loud it was probably heard in the nearby village.

"Oops!" she laughed, rolling off the floor. "Sorry, Bishop. Don' know my own strength."

The Bishop, trying to remain dignified, abruptly stood. He seemed like he was about to say something, but instead smoothed back his black hair and sat down without saying a word.

Lucy's eyes went wide with surprise. She'd never seen her father at a loss for words before. Her surprise was interrupted though, when her stomach began to churn, giving off a loud gurgle. She hadn't realized she was so hungry. Lucy picked out a delicious looking piece of fruit with shiny red seeds in it and was trying to pry one of them loose when all of a sudden it popped with force, sending juice cross the table and into Eugene's face.

"Yeh did that on purpose," he grumbled, wiping the red juice from his cheeks.

"If I'd done it on purpose, there would be more than a squirt between your eyes," Lucy declared proudly.

Maybe Mrs. McBeal felt sorry for her son, or perhaps she just wanted to announce the day's schedule, but when the laughing soared it was Eugene's mother who quickly changed the mood to a serious one. "I'm pleased that yeh all find that entertainin', but we have the order of the day ter discuss," she said sharply. That was when it became obvious to Lucy that Mrs. McBeal was not a force to be reckoned with.

"Bishop Tuppins," Mrs. McBeal said in a more cordial conversational tone, "I've engaged a very fine and outstandin' island boy from the village ter serve as a guide today fer the children."

Eugene quickly responded, hoping to regain his respect as the eldest boy, "Splendid idea, Mam." He looked across the table at Lucy and smiled with a hint of mischief in his eyes.

"My daughter is not accustomed to the rigors of island life," protested the Bishop.

"I assure yeh that Kalani is very responsible. He has taken Eugene and Oliver many times to pick *guavas* fer our pantry," said Mrs. McBeal.

Oliver spoke while still chewing a mouthful of biscuit. "Yum. Makes wonderful jam. Here, yeh want some?" offering another biscuit slathered with jam to Bishop Tuppins.

"Well, it probably would do Lucy a world of good to stretch those legs of hers," relented the Bishop.

"Eugene," advised Mrs. McBeal, "yeh need ter watch out fer Lucy since Elizabeth has ter help me today."

Lucy dropped her fork onto the plate. She couldn't believe her ears. Didn't she have any say in what she got to do today? "Elizabeth's not coming?" she asked. "Papa! I can take care of myself and don't need Eugene watching over me."

The Bishop gave her a worried look and said, "It's just that I know you will be tempted to pick up every bug you see. There are dangers in the jungle, Lucy."

"Insects. Not bugs!" she corrected, folding her arms across her chest.

"Right!" interrupted Mrs. McBeal, once more taking charge of the conversation. "It's all settled. So everybody be ready by ten o'clock. Come along, Eugene. We've got ter collect a few things."

The group begun to disperse but Lucy remained at the table. She was stunned at the fact that she had no control over her own fate for the day. She had hoped that she would be able to explore the garden behind the house. Now Eugene was going to make trouble and spoil everything, she just knew it.

In the doorway Eugene turned to look at Lucy. He gave her the silent stare he knew would irritate her. Then he smirked before turning to follow after his mother, relishing in his first triumph over Lucy.

Deep into the jungle Kalani led the children. He carried a large knife that came in handy when clearing the overgrown leaves away from the path.

Oliver and Eugene knew to stay close to Kalani from previous experience. The jungle wasn't a safe place to be if you weren't careful. But Lucy was taking her time and kept strolling off the path.

"Come along, Lucy. We haven' all day!" called out Eugene, looking for her blonde curls above the foliage.

She was walking stooped down in a heavily wooded area when she heard him and stood straight up, getting a face full of the cool mountain breeze. She was wearing the ugly garment that Mrs. McBeal had made for her. It wasn't at all comfortable and the sweat on her skin made it horribly itchy. Lucy paused a moment to scratch her stomach. Her purse was tied around her waist, so she had to twist and turn it to get to the irritated spot.

"Just hold onto your britches, Eugene!" she hollered back. It was then that she spotted a roach the size of a small bird. She stopped and pulled out her pencil and paper, excitedly making a sketch of her latest discovery.

Meanwhile, Kalani and the boys had kept walking. They didn't realize that Lucy wasn't catching up to them until they turned around and saw her tiny figure crouched down near the ground far behind them.

"Honestly, Lucy!" yelled Eugene in a louder voice this time. "Catch up with us!"

"I'm fine!" she called back. "Just drawing something. I'll be there in a minute!"

Lucy was just putting the antennae on the beetle when a drop of sweat fell on the paper. "Blasts!" She tried to quickly blot it up with the corner of her traveling dress, but groaned when part of her sketch got ruined.

Oliver came running out of the bushes, then startling Lucy before disappearing again into the brush. She was sure that he was just being silly while reminding her to hurry along. She looked up and called out to the boys, "I'm finished now! Wait up!"

But they were too far ahead to hear her. As she scurried down along the pathway, she noticed orange and yellow looking balls of fruit. Lucy dodged them at first, but the path soon became a smashed fruit slime-covered trail, and there was no way she could avoid stepping on any of it. Suddenly, both of her feet slid in opposite directions, sending her down into the muck.

"Ouch!" Lucy cried out, jerking her hand out of the slimy pulp. Surprised and curious, she carefully felt for the hard object that had poked her palm when she fell. After wiping off the *guava* slime, Lucy realized that she held a shiny stone in her hand. She stared at it for a moment in disbelief. It was a bright red gem the size of a plum.

"Lucy!" Kalani sounded faintly in the distance. "Where are you?"

"Coming!" she replied, hiding the jewel in her purse. She didn't want Eugene taking it from her.

Despite the odor of rotting fruit, there was a sense of peace that filled Lucy as she walked by herself along the path. The maze of huge leaves and rock walls surrounding her reminded her of the English forest where she and her grandmother hunted for berries.

When she came around a huge wall of boulders she abruptly stopped dead in her tracks. Just one more step and Lucy would have found herself ankle deep in a streambed.

"There you are," said Kalani, standing several feet away on the opposite bank.

"No way!" objected Lucy staring at the shiny gray stones flickering under the flowing water. "I'm not crossing that!"

"There's nothing to it! Now, just take it slow and step around the rocks. It's not very deep," Kalani assured her, reaching out with his hand.

High on a ledge beyond Kalani she spotted someone looking down at them. She knew that it wasn't an islander because he was fully dressed in dark clothing, but he was so far away that she couldn't make out who it was. She got a bad feeling in her gut then that he meant trouble.

Eugene's voice shouted from up ahead, "Hey, Kalani. I could have told yeh she'd be scared ter cross. Scaredy-cat, Lucy!"

When Lucy looked back up to the ledge, the dark figure was gone. She sighed at the whole situation, then decided that she needed to show Eugene he was wrong. *Confidence, that's what Elizabeth call it,* Lucy remembered. She was going to be confident. So she lifted the hemline of the traveling dress with one hand and covered her purse with the other while she touched the water tentatively with the tip of her shoe.

She heard Kalani's soft reassuring voice, but it was no use. The minute the coldness seeped into her shoe, her throat closed up and she couldn't breathe. She was gasping for air when Kalani rushed across the water and lifted her into his arms.

"Don't worry, Lucy. Elizabeth told me to take good care of you," he said as he carried her the rest of the way to the waterfall.

Ten

A Gold Coin

The roar of the water was worse than a train's locomotive. Lucy covered her ears, but she couldn't even muffle out the noise.

Kalani had left her on the bank of the pool. He and the boys dove in and out of the frothy water enjoying its coolness.

Lucy looked up overhead. The falls were gushing over the cliff through a maze of giant ferns growing out of the rockface. The water had traveled downhill from the top of *Haleakala* mountain, picking up speed until it hit the outcropping that hung over the large cave in front of where Lucy sat. She silently watched as the silvery droplets splashed off the stones before plummeting into the dark water.

"Come in," invited Eugene.

"Aye, it's refreshing ter the soul," added Oliver, treading water next to his brother.

"I'm refreshed, thank you," Lucy replied, tucking her thumbs under the purse strap.

"Bet yeh she can't swim," Eugene commented to Oliver.

"I can swim just fine. Just don't feel like it, that's all," she said defensively.

Seeing Lucy alone on a rock, Kalani came up out of the water and took her by the hand. He led the little girl around the pool and under the ledge into a cave.

"This is Elizabeth's favorite spot," he told her, turning to leave. "It is quiet in here."

"Thank you," Lucy called after him, climbing up onto a dry boulder. She removed the strap around her waist and placed her purse on the rock, but it slipped to the ground.

"Blasts!" she said, bending down to retrieve the purse. She felt something jump onto her shoulder and much to her delight, noticed it was a small shiny green lizard.

"Why, hello there!" she greeted the visitor. "Come to watch me?" The gecko was unconcerned by the girl and continued to remain perched on her shoulder while she continued to look for her purse. Lucy secretly hoped she would be able to take him home for her collection. As she felt the dark ground around the boulder, her fingers touched something hard just below the mud.

The brown guck was no obstacle to Lucy and she pulled the object out with ease. She cleaned off the mud to reveal a gold coin.

"Hey, Lucy," called Eugene. "Are yeh hidin' in there?"

Lucy spotted her purse just then and snatched it up, depositing the coin within. She knew she had to keep her discoveries a secret from Eugene if she wanted to hold onto the coin and gem, so she tucked the purse under a dry rock nearby. Much to her disappointment, the gecko decided to jump off her shoulder and scamper up the cave wall.

"Really, Eugene," she sighed, "I'm coming!"

Kalani met her just outside the cave and took one look at her shoes covered in guck. "Rinse them off in the water. Here, hold my hand and I'll steady you."

"My shoes are just fine the way they are," she said backing away from Kalani. Lucy had no intention of even touching just the surface of the pool's water.

"Watch out fer critters under the water," warned Eugene teasingly, waving his hand back and forth on the surface.

Then Oliver joined in the ruse, and they were both splashing. "Aye, when yeh see the wee red thin's, watch out."

"For your information," announced Lucy, "I'm not afraid of little critters." The water frightened her much more than any of God's creatures.

Indignantly, she reached out for Kalani's hand and he led her into the shallow of the water. Lucy took a deep breath getting ready for the fear to flood her chest. But it didn't come. She couldn't believe what had just happened, she was standing in moving water and felt – soothing. Kalani smiled at her and let go of her hand before diving under the water.

Lucy looked down and saw her pale knees glowing from their paleness. She giggled at the tiny red shrimp tickling her skin as they encircled her legs.

Then, she had an idea. She was almost certain that it would prove to be both a test of Eugene's courage and amusing Oliver.

Lucy stifled a grin and began to point to the water, shouting out, "I felt something!"

"Where?" said Oliver in alarm.

"Must have been two feet long," she replied frantically, continuing with the farce, "and brushed right pass me, too!" She remained in the water trying to look frightened. But as soon as the two boys scampered out of the water, Lucy broke out into a contagious laugh.

"Yeh could have stopped my heart!" Eugene complained, giving Lucy one of his cold stares as he wrapped up in a blanket.

Oliver was laughing through his chattering teeth. "Well, I thought it was grand, Lucy. Didn' know yeh had it in yeh."

Lucy smiled from ear to ear, for she knew she had won the game this time.

Eleven

The Warning

The day is shaping up to be pretty good, thought Lucy. She'd discovered a new insect, found two new trinkets, and managed to outwit Eugene.

Oliver grabbed hold of a hanging vine and swung over a large boulder to impress her.

"Hey, try this!" he said, landing several feet in front of her.

"I'll pass," she waved him off. "I think you've been doing that for some time and it takes some skill."

Lucy thought it looked like fun, but she figured that Oliver's technique was learned, probably by trial and error, and she was content to merely observe instead of breaking her neck.

The foursome continued through the forest until Lucy wandered away, catching sight of a cockroach jumping off a mango in the middle of the path. One more step and she might have squashed it flat with her shoe! She gasped at the thought.

Sensing the large girl, the creature flew to a rotten stump a few feet away, tucking brown wings neatly onto its back as it settled on the spot. The body of the roach reminded her of a shiny armor shield. *Wow,* she thought, *this would be a terrific specimen to add to my collection.* She tried to catch it, but it had been watching out for her and escaped onto another log.

When Lucy realized she wasn't going to be able to capture it, she decided a drawing of the cockroach would have to do. She removed her purse and took out her pencil and paper, then snuck up to the insect, placing the pouch on a nearby log. She bent down to get a better look when she bumped the purse, spilling its contents on the ground. "Blasts!" she complained.

A large shadow moved over the trinkets and she knew then that she wasn't alone. She looked up to see who it was, but the sun blotted out the details of the man's face. Lucy recognized him though when she smelled the familiar stench of cigar smoke. She tried to run away but felt Burles' fingers dig into her skin and lift her into the air.

"Oh, stop your squirming," the big man pulled down stared at her with stone-cold green eyes.

"Let me go!" shouted Lucy.

"Listen up, youngster. Never can tell when a dangerous creature could appear in these woods. The kind that could tear you apart like sliced bacon."

Lucy didn't take his warning. She thought it was all a bluff to scare her, talking of wild creatures with teeth and sharp claws. It was preposterous. Besides, her heart was leaping inside her chest and right then she was more afraid of him than anything else.

Burles held her dangling by both arms now. "Young girls have no business in this jungle. Mind you, little Lady, this is not England."

Then Lucy heard Eugene's voice in the distance. She never thought she'd be so glad to hear him, but at that moment she was.

"Come on Lucy, where are yeh?" he called out, getting closer.

When Lucy's captor set her down on the ground, she spied the gold coin nearby and slowly slid her foot over it pretending to edge away from him. He'd taken the coin she'd found on the ship, but she was determined that he wouldn't get this one.

"Daddy's little princess, ha!" mocked the man. "You won't be any good to him if you get yourself mauled to death." And with that remark, he disappeared into the thick trees.

Lucy retrieved the coin from under her shoe. She scooped everything up by the log and shoved it all into her purse just in time, too, because Kalani appeared soon after.

"There you are!" he said, relieved.

"Yeh cannot go out on yehr own like that," reprimanded Eugene, coming up behind their guide.

Oliver caught up to the group and tugged at Lucy's dress. "Did yeh see any interestin' bugs?" he asked.

"Oliver, they are-" began Lucy, scowling at her friend. "How many times do I have to tell you-"

"Insects," Oliver corrected himself before she could finish. "Sorry."

Kalani took Lucy by the hand and hustled her along the path. This time he seemed irritated and said, "We'd better make some good time if we are going to get back by night fall."

"Hey, Lucy," said Oliver, "show me yehr drawin'."

Eugene looked back at Lucy and snorted loudly. He disliked her wasting their time and didn't want her to delay them any longer.

"Oliver, did you know that famous scientists are famous because they take risks?" she began her litany, glancing up at Eugene now and then. "Risks that take them where the unknown is fantastic and unconceivable."

"Aye, but the unknown here can get yeh killed," Eugene muttered.

"What about the drawin?" Oliver repeated, tugging at her leather purse from behind.

"Later, Oliver," she said as Kalani quickened their pace. "The wait will be worth it. Believe me!"

Twelve

MENEHUNE

The jungle was a mysterious place to Lucy. It seemed to go on forever as they walked the winding path in search of the guava forest. Kalani had let go of Lucy's hand and resumed the lead. And being the curious girl she was, she lagged behind a little from constantly surveying her surroundings.

She noticed leaves the size of elephant's ears blocking out the sunlight. She also had a nagging feeling that someone was following them, but when she turned she only saw trees. Then she felt something brush the top of her head. When she looked up, she saw that the trees had bent sideways and all their branches where swaying above her head. *Am I dreaming,* she thought. Frightened, she started running to catch up with the others.

"Do you suppose there are giants that live in this jungle?" she asked Oliver, who was now just a little ways ahead of her.

When she turned around again to check, she thought she saw the trees straighten back to the sky.

"Nope," replied the boy, "Haven't heard about any giants."

"Can't you move any faster?" she urged, prodding Oliver in the back. "We're so far behind Eugene and Kalani."

"Don' worry. I know where we're goin'."

"Maybe there is a giant up in that cave," Lucy began speculating. Her eyes lingered on the cave entrance as they passed it. "He could be anywhere at all, just lurking through the trees, and we'd never know it," she teased.

"Nope," Oliver replied simply. "Just *Menehune,* the wee people."

"Sorry?"

Oliver paused briefly to look back at Lucy. "Yeh know, the wee people."

"Oliver," she sighed deeply, and shoved him forward, "if you want to scare me with your tales then you'll have to do better than that."

"But it's true, I promise," he said, walking onward. "I got lost once. Then I found some wee stones leading me all the way out of the forest. That's what *Menehune* do. They help yeh when yeh are lost."

"You mean to tell me there are leprechauns here on the island?" Lucy asked skeptically.

"Are yeh daft, lassie? I said *Menehune!*"

"No, I'm not daft. I just think that it's not very nice of you to lie to me. I thought we were friends," she pouted, feeling a little betrayed by her comrade. They turned a corner and Lucy perked up. "There – up ahead! I see Kalani."

Lucy forged ahead but Oliver continued to trail behind, telling his stories.

"Did yeh know some forty years ago, we'd be standin' right in the path of flowin' lava? Came shootin' right out of the top of that mountain, it did."

"Lava?" asked Lucy, glancing back.

"Aye, hot stuff. And when it hit the forest floor, gas and air were trapped. Lucky fer us, too. It made all these grand tunnels around here."

"You seem to know a lot. Did Elizabeth teach you?"

Oliver shook his head. "Oh, she wouldn't teach us that sort of thin'. The islanders are the ones I learned it from. They've told me many stories. They even told me about all the honeycombed tunnels that are on this side of the island."

Just in front of Lucy was an entrance to one of the tunnels. It looked very dark inside and she had no intention of exploring it on her own.

Thirteen

MRS. McBEAL

Later that afternoon, Lucy stood in the kitchen, scratching her belly through the ugly garment. Mrs. McBeal was pleased with the bags of guava fruit the children had gathered and helped Lucy and Kalani sort the bruised ones from the good ones.

"Lucy, dear," she advised the itchy girl, "why don' yeh run upstairs and change."

When Mrs. McBeal arrived on the island, the islanders had never seen a person from England or any other part of the world. There was no proper house for the new missionaries and they had to live in a grass covered hut with a dirt floor.

Mrs. McBeal worked hard tilling the land with her hands, planting seeds and growing a vegetable garden. Sometimes insects nibbled on the new plants during the late night hours, and Mrs. McBeal would have to start all over with her planting. But she was never discouraged, and with her strong faith, she was confident that God would provide what they needed.

"Heavens," she remarked to Kalani, "look at all this fruit. It is truly a blessin' from the Lord above."

"Yes, mam," he replied.

Lucy quickly shed her damp clothes in the solitude of her bedroom and slid into a soft cotton dress. She couldn't wait to polish the gold coin and add it to her trinket collection so she fished it out of her leather purse. It had to be worth a lot of money because there was a picture of the Queen stamped on top.

A knock at the door startled Lucy from her thoughts and she tucked the coin back into the purse on her pillow.

"Hello," announced Elizabeth, coming in and sitting on the other side of the bed. "Well, tell me, how was the pool?"

"I gave Eugene quite a fright," reported Lucy with a satisfied smile.

"Aye, I heard. He'll be on his guard now, so be careful," cautioned Elizabeth.

Lucy felt her eyelids get heavy and she realized she was exhausted from the long hike in the forest so she slid under her blanket and rested her head on the pillow. When the elder girl looked at her in surprise, Lucy groaned, "I'm tired, Elizabeth. Every bit of my energy gone – poof!" She shut her eyes to go to sleep.

Elizabeth yanked on the pillow. "Yeh know," she informed the sleepy girl, "there's a party tonight. And yeh are expected ter attend."

"I'm not going," said Lucy, peeking open an eye for one second, "Can't you see that my arms and legs have already said good night?" She took a deep breath and stretched out her sore limbs, draping them over the sides of the mattress to dangle in the air.

"That's nice dear. But yeh have ter come. It's in honor of yehr father."

Elizabeth continued to explain that when the Chief commanded a party, everyone had to attend. There would be singing and dancing, and a huge feast called a *luau*. She patted Lucy on the head, taking the little girls silence as assurance she would go.

"I'll comb out yehr curls if yeh'd like," offered Elizabeth.

"That's nice," Lucy replied, yawning and falling asleep on her comfy pillow.

Lucy didn't know for how long she had dozed off, but when she opened her eyes she heard muffled words coming from Reverend McBeal's study.

The voices speaking were harsh and arguing over something important.

She slipped quietly down the stairs and sat on the bottom step next to the closed doors of the study. After a minute of lingering, she could distinguish their voices: her father,

Oliver's father, and Reverend Machesney heatedly discussing church plans.

Then she heard one other voice that hushed the others with a commanding tone. "Listen up, guvnor," the voice called out, "you were the one that came to me in England. Begging, you were, to have someone like me to carry out your plans."

Lucy recognized who it was. Although she didn't remember his name, she knew it was the cigar smoking man. Just the thought of him brought a shiver up her spine.

"But we didn't agree on this," protested the Bishop. Lucy had never heard her father talk like this. She crept closer to the door, worried for him.

"All I know is I'm the one in charge. You do it my way, or I'm done with it right here and now."

There was a scuffle of chairs and suddenly all four were talking at once. Then she heard the deep tone of Reverend Machesney's voice continue the conversation. "There's too much at stake ter get behind now. In less than six months the doctor and printer will be arrivin', and we have ter stick ter the time line."

"I'll get those islanders into shape, if it's the last thing I do," the cigar smoking man said in a threatening voice. Lucy then feared that her father had hired a dangerous man.

"You must assure me that no one will be hurt," insisted the Bishop.

"Guvnor, it's nothing that you need to concern yourself about," the man replied.

Before Bishop Tuppins could say something else, Reverend Machesney cut in, "Then it's settled. We all have the same deadline."

"Just making sure we understand each other," protested the Bishop.

Lucy had her ear pressed against the door. Gray curls of sickening cigar smoke started wafting through the opening near the floor, so she quickly covered her nose and mouth to keep from gagging. She watched as their shadows moved under the door, pacing back and forth.

"Just have the money ready when I come to collect, and leave the rest to me," demanded the man.

"I don' know about this, Bishop," warned Reverend McBeal, his voice uneasy. "Spent two years buildin' the Chief's trust, I have. Gettin' his permission ter expand the mission into a settlement took a lot of delicate negotiatin'. Aye, and yeh don' want ter mess with that chap, believe me."

"I need to think about this," said Lucy's father, wearily. "Reverend McBeal has a valid point. The Chief plays a vital role in our progress here."

Lucy heard footsteps coming closer to the door and her heart sounded loudly in her ears. Then she saw the door knob turn. She bolted up the steps and hid behind the posts in the balcony, trying to get a good look at the cigar man's face as he left the room.

"Either you want the buildings built, or you don't," the man called over his shoulder as he walked to the front door. "I didn't come all this way not to finish the job."

"You'll get your money, don't worry," assured the Bishop from inside the study.

"I'd better. It would be most unfortunate to find someone you love at the bottom of the gulch," muttered the man, exiting the house.

Shocked at what she'd just heard, Lucy suddenly gasped in so much air that she almost choked. She ran into her room, slid out the window, and clung to a branch of the climbing tree to make sure he left. But he'd already disappeared into the forest.

Fourteen

The Luau

J ust after sunset, the Chief sat among his inner circle ad-
visors and in front of them a feast of food was displayed
on a *tapa cloth*. A platform had been built to raise the royal
leader higher than everyone else. The women and children
were not allowed to sit and eat with the Chief. Lucy watched
him from across the clearing and didn't like the fact that in
comparison she, Eugene, and Oliver had to sit on the hard
ground.

The entertainment for the evening featured none other
than Kalani and eight dark-skinned dancers, swooping up
and down with quick, fluid movements that looked fierce
and warlike. The fast beating of rhythms filled the air as the
musicians' slapped their palms against dried *umeke* gourds.
As the dancers approached Lucy's mat, she held her breath.

Kalani seemed harmless, but after the strange happenings earlier today on the path she wondered if it was really safe on the island.

"Eugene," she asked, turning to talk to someone and get her mind off the dancers, "What do the words of the song mean?"

"It's not really a song; they call it *hula*. The dance tells a story," he explained, picking up a coconut and draining the cloudy juice into his gaping mouth.

"That's disgusting," she said, watching the liquid dribble down his chin. "Have you lost all your proper manners? And do you know the story or not!" she added impatiently when he ignored her.

Eugene laughed. "Probably an old one," he added.

"How old?" she asked.

"A lot older than father is," chimed in Oliver. "Besides, they say there are thousands of stories of their ancestors. Bet yeh there are even millions and trillions."

"Good Lord, Oliver," said Eugene, rolling his eyes. "Stop exaggerating so."

Lucy was growing bored. She wanted to get up and go back to the house where she could read a book or polish her coin. But no one could leave the *luau* without the Chief's permission. Since her father was the guest of honor she definitely couldn't go. Lucy sighed and was looking around absently when something new caught her attention; torch lights high up on the mountain.

"What's that?" she asked.

"The *heiau*," answered Oliver seeing where she was pointing. "Yeh saw it earlier today. The place with the heads."

"It looks different in the dark. Have you ever been up there?" she inquired further, happy to have found something interesting to talk about.

"It's *kapu*. That means forbidden."

"Oh, but I bet that doesn't mean that we couldn't go up there. It might be fun to explore. Maybe you could show me tomorrow," suggested Lucy.

"Not me," Oliver shook his head vigorously. "It's a holy place where the Chief's ancestors used ter have sacrifices. They came from the island of Tahiti and followed the stars all the way here in canoes, *wa'a*. Yeh don' want ter go there, Lucy. They cut off people's heads up there."

"Oh!" she replied, putting her hand to her mouth in shock.

Just then, Lucy's stomach grumbled from hunger. She hadn't eaten but a few *guava* on the journey into the forest with the boys earlier that day.

"Papa, I'm hungry. When can I eat?" she asked.

But her father was intrigued by the display of women wiggling and shaking their legs to the rhythms of the music, and eating was very far from his thoughts.

"Not now, Lucy. Be patient," he responded, still staring at the dancers.

Patience was not something Lucy felt interested in at that very moment. Her stomach ached, her body was tired, and she was bored of just sitting around on a mat. She wasn't the sort of girl who tried to be bad. Usually, it was her imagination that got her into trouble. So she tried to behave like her father wanted, crossing her legs and staring into the crowd, attempting to be patient.

That was when she noticed Elizabeth was gone missing. Lucy excused herself, saying she needed to stretch her legs, and set out behind the huts to find her friend. A scream nearby cut through the sounds of the *luau* music. It was Elizabeth. Lucy hurriedly searched between each hut but she couldn't find her friend.

When she spotted Reverend Machesney she was about to call for help. He was leaning into a palm tree. She couldn't make out what he was doing, so she approached cautiously to ask him if he'd seen Elizabeth.

He heard her footsteps and turned around. To Lucy's horror, she saw her friend sitting on a stump, blood trickling down the side of her neck.

"Oh, Elizabeth!" Lucy cried. She pushed the clergyman away and took Elizabeth's hand.

"It's alright, dear," the elder girl assured Lucy. "And it was a good thin' the Reverend was near. I was lookin' down at the baking pit here and one of the torches fell and hit me from behind."

"Aye, it was a good thin'," repeated the Reverend. He put his arm firmly around Elizabeth's waist and helped her up. "There's no tellin' what could have happened. Here, let me help yeh back ter the *luau*."

Lucy was suspicious that the Reverend was far too comfortable holding Elizabeth. So, the little girl nudged her body between them and insisted, "If there's going to be any escorting, then I'm going to do it. Come, Elizabeth. I'll help you."

The Reverend continued to hover over Elizabeth. Finally, the elder girl stood and said, "I'm fine, Reverend Machesney. Yeh go on back now, we can manage without yeh."

The clergyman scowled at Lucy, but did not argue. Lucy watched him return to the *luau* celebration. Then she turned to Elizabeth.

"Are you really okay?" she asked, full of worry.

Elizabeth smiled gratefully. "Aye. It all just happened so fast."

Lucy examined the other nearby torches. They were all set in deep holes. It just didn't make any sense that one of them would have fallen on its own. A sudden thought struck her: what if the Reverend had purposely struck Elizabeth so that he could pretend to help her? A chill ran up her spine at the thought of what he might have done next while alone with Elizabeth. She decided to keep her ideas to herself, but from now on she would look out for her friend.

"What's down there anyway?" Lucy wondered aloud.

"They're roasting a pig," replied Elizabeth.

"No! exclaimed Lucy in amazement. She peered down into the pit expecting to see a pig, but all she saw were long green leaves and steamy hot stones.

"Aye. Wrapped up like a babe in a buntin'. Yeh've never tasted anythin' so marvelous," said Elizabeth wide-eyed.

Something behind Elizabeth caught Lucy's attention. It moved quickly in the darkness. She grabbed Elizabeth's hand in a panic to pull her away, but was relieved when it was only Kalani who popped out from behind a palm tree.

"Takin' an awful chance, yeh are," warned Elizabeth, quietly staring into the pit.

"I had to see you," he whispered, walking up next to her and setting his gaze on the pit.

Lucy realized that they must be good friends to be talking like this. She stood on the other side of Elizabeth, still holding her hand.

Kalani leaned forward to look around Elizabeth. "Aloha, Lucy," he said.

"That means hello," translated Elizabeth.

"Is it true that there's a pig down there?" asked Lucy.

"Yes," he answered. "Early in the morning, my friends and I went into the valley and caught *pua'a* for *luau* for your father. He is a very important person to us; a teacher."

"Kalani is son of the Chief, Lucy," explained Elizabeth.

"Really?" Lucy turned to Kalani and gave him a curtsy. "And here I thought you were just a guide. Imagine that, you are royalty like a King and Queen. That makes you a prince."

Elizabeth chuckled. "I can see that yeh have quite the imagination." She couldn't help but laugh at Lucy's wild thoughts. "Kalani is descended from Ki'i, a great ruling chief of Tahiti. Ki'i sailed here on a canoe hundreds of years ago."

"The village of Kalhikinui on the Big Island means great Tahiti," he added.

"You don't talk like the others," Lucy said when she noticed that Kalani spoke very good English.

"He's been learnin' English at the mission school. Catchin' on quite well, don' yeh think?" asked Elizabeth proudly.

"Then I will see you again. Perhaps at the school?" hoped Lucy.

"Certainly not!" Elizabeth cut in. "Yeh see, I will be teachin' yeh up at the house along with Eugene and Oliver."

"What?" Lucy exclaimed confusedly. "Not a proper school?" She was surprised. After all, she'd always attended a classroom full of students her own age when they lived in England. It never crossed her mind that she wouldn't be walking to a school house every morning like before.

Elizabeth explained patiently. "It is proper, Lucy. The islanders learn how to spell and speak English at the missionary school. Since we already know all that, we will learn other thin's at the house."

"Just Eugene and Oliver?" Lucy asked, still unsure. "Doesn't seem proper to me."

How could it be a real school with just the three of us? she thought. *And Eugene one of the three!* She couldn't bear to put up with his disapproving stares all day.

"Don' concern yehrself with school on this fine evenin'," sighed Elizabeth.

"I've got to get back," murmured Kalani, stealing a glance into Elizabeth's eyes.

"Tomorrow then, in the village. I'll meet yeh behind the canoe hut at noon," Elizabeth whispered with a blush.

"Pleasure to make your acquaintance, Lucy," said Kalani, waving her goodbye.

"Farewell, sweet prince," the little girl replied admiringly, bowing down and finishing with, "and until we meet again."

Kalani grinned from ear to ear. He was flattered. "Just Kalani, little *keiki*," he responded.

Elizabeth tugged Lucy along, leading her back to the feast.

"So yeh're an actress, huh," she said, amused by her new pupil. "I'll be sure ter remember that."

Fifteen

THREE GIFTS

When Lucy and Elizabeth returned to the celebration, they found the Bishop wasn't all too pleased that his daughter had been missing.

"Where have you two been?" he scolded.

"Papa," said Lucy, "you wouldn't believe your eyes! There's a pig wrapped up in leaves and it's cooking in a hole!"

The Bishop raised one eyebrow and looked questionably at Elizabeth.

"Oh, it's quite sanitary, sir. I can assure yeh of that."

"Lucy, you've missed out on some important introductions," he added. "Don't go wandering off again, do you understand?"

"Yes, Papa," she replied, lowering her head in compliance.

Before setting out on their trip, Lucy and her father had gone shopping for special gifts to give to the McBeal family.

The feast was the first chance the Bishop had to formally present the gifts and he reached under his coat and pulled them out of his pocket.

"Lucy," he said, "I think this is a fine time to show our hosts the gifts that we brought them."

"Yes, yes," she agreed, sliding closer to her father.

"Eugene," called the Bishop, reaching into his hand and holding up a watch with gold chain. "I hear that you are a lad who takes pride in being punctual."

"Aye, sir," replied Eugene. "A fine Scottish gentleman keeps ter his word when he says he will be at a given place and time."

"True. Well, our family would like you to accept this gift." The Bishop reached over and placed the watch into Eugene's hand.

"Oh, thank yeh, sir. It's splendid," he said, admiring the time piece.

"Lucy, why don't you present the next gift," the Bishop proposed, placing a small brass case in the palm of her hand.

"And for you Oliver," Lucy spoke loudly over the sounds of the music, "we understand you are a boy who often wanders about in the forest."

"I don' wander," the young boy argued.

"Mind yehr manners, Oliver," reminded Mrs. McBeal. "Continue, dear."

"Here is a compass so that you may always find your way home safely," Lucy finished, handing him the case.

"Mam, I don' get lost!" protested Oliver to deaf ears.

"Does give me fright at times, this wee lad," Mrs. McBeal remarked to the Bishop, ruffling the fuzzy mop on Oliver's head.

"Besides the *Menehune* always show me the way," Oliver continued quietly opening the case and staring at the pointer on the compass.

"Oliver, yeh know that yeh mustn' be tellin' tales," cautioned Elizabeth.

"And for you, Elizabeth," said the Bishop, "A fine tortoise shell comb." He reached past his young assistant, Reverend Machesney and placed the comb into the girl's hand.

Elizabeth was thrilled and immediately reached up to pull down her hair when the comb slipped out of her hand.

"Here yeh are," said Reverend Machesney, picking the comb up and securing it into her cascading locks. "It compliments yehr lovely tresses."

Lucy noticed Elizabeth's brightly blushing cheeks. It was not proper for a man to touch a young woman in public as he had touched Elizabeth.

The *luau* feast was the grandest party the Chief had ever organized. Thousands of islanders had come to meet the new missionary. The dancing and singing went on for many hours while the Chief and his friends got drunk. Lucy stuffed herself after all that waiting.

Mrs. McBeal was not happy with the Chief's behavior because she and her husband had spent many hours discussing the dangers of drink with the ruler.

The Chief was sitting a long ways off, but Lucy saw that he was laughing and drinking with a large man, groomed and wearing a fine silk suit.

"Papa, who is that?" she asked, pointing to the stranger.

But her father was too busy talking to Reverend Machesney and ignored his daughter. She began to eavesdrop on what Mrs. McBeal and her husband were saying which proved to offer some sort of explanation.

"Well, dear," Mrs. McBeal was saying, "it's just a sacrilege. Don' yeh agree, husband? Look at the way he is carryin' on."

"The Lord works in mysterious ways," Reverend McBeal replied.

"Well, what is the Bishop ter make of all this?" she asked worriedly.

"Isn't it true that yeh have taught the Chief many fine social graces? So have patience, my dear wife."

"You have done a good work here," said the Bishop, turning to the couple and joining their conversation. "I understand the Chief has professed a strong desire to love God."

"It's true, he has," reassured the Reverend McBeal. "However, there still seems ter be the matter of his many women."

Lucy had been wondering why those women sat far behind the Chief, and now she noticed that none of them had picked up anything to eat yet. "Mrs. McBeal," asked Lucy, "why don't the Chief's women eat with him?"

"They forbid it," she answered, glancing sideways at the girl. "Now can yeh imagine a Scotsman tellin' his wife that she couldn't partake in the meal that she slaved over a hot stove ter prepare fer him? Ha! And just look at the Chief now, taken up the drink again." Mrs. McBeal shook her head in disapproval.

"I'm sure the Church is most pleased with your teachings here," the Bishop said to Mrs. McBeal. "Is it true that the Chief was inquiring about the destruction of heaven and earth at the final judgment?"

"He should be more concerned about his own judgment, I would think," commented Mrs. McBeal, picking up a piece of pineapple from the platter. "Look at all those silks on those women! The man in the suit givin' the Chief rum, and wasn't he at our house today?"

"Oh yes, ma'am. He's -," the young Reverend Machesney began to speak, but the Bishop held up his hand and cut the reply short. He cleared his throat.

"Ambition can be a fine virtue, or it can destroy a young man's path to success," warned the Bishop, looking directly at his young assistant. "I'd think about your place amongst this congregation before contributing to a conversation of your elders."

Lucy was shocked at her father's words. She had assumed that the diocese sent Reverend Machesney to accompany her father because they wanted to keep an eye on the mission. But it was apparent that the young reverend had no authority.

The Bishop then turned and lifted Lucy protectively onto his lap. She was pleased to feel his kind touch once again.

Maybe the island was a good place for him. She wrapped her arms around his neck.

"Lucy, dear," he spoke into her ear, "the name of the man in the suit is Burles, remember. And I have secured his services for the mission's building expansion. You will be seeing a lot of him. But stay out of his way, do you understand?"

Lucy understood more than her father knew. She had heard Burles' threat clear as day earlier that afternoon. And she didn't want to end up at the bottom of the gulch.

Sixteen

The Secret

The white clapboard house surrounded by long swaying field grass was more than just the home for the Tuppins and McBeal families. It had the only library on the island, the only classroom that had a table and chairs for the missionary children, and a formal office where the clergymen could conduct business.

But to Lucy, the house was first and foremost her home. She loved her spacious bedroom the most. The sweet aromas coming out of the kitchen reminded her of her own mother's cooking. And the porch became her second favorite spot because she and her father watched the colors of the sunset every night burst across the blue sky.

Her school desk was the dining room table. It was made from a smooth golden hardwood and stretched down the entire length of the dining area. At night it was covered with fresh baked goods, fruits, and vegetables for the evening meal; but during the day it served as a classroom desk for Eugene, Oliver, and Lucy.

She still didn't like the fact that she wasn't in a formal school with other girls her age. Most days it was hard for her to concentrate on her studies. She found herself staring out at the banana groves swaying in the breeze. And Elizabeth's lessons were not challenging enough since Lucy had learned much of England's history while attending the Ebley school the year before.

It didn't take very long for her to also become aware that the house was not quite a secure place. There were too many people just coming and going out of the house all day. Lucy didn't trust her trinket collection to be unattended while she was in class. Any one of the servants or adults could wander in and search through her room, so she kept the coin and gem tucked in her purse. And every day she was vigilant in tying the purse around her waist so she knew exactly where her trinkets would be.

"Elizabeth, I'm finished with my journal entry," announced Lucy. "Can I join the boys in the study?"

"Doin' research, lassie?" asked Elizabeth, as she nodded. "Yeh've the makin's of a fine student, Lucy."

Lucy liked Elizabeth more and more. Elizabeth's favorite subject was Math and assigned daily homework sheets, but Lucy did not particularly like having to solve division problems. Although the elder girl was only sixteen, Lucy thought that Elizabeth carried herself with the grace and poise of a noble lady.

The study was a huge library room. It was directly across the entrance hall from the dining room and housed a great number of books and volumes. Reverend McBeal had the collection shipped over after the house had been built, and now the various publications were lined up neat and orderly on shelves that reached to the ceiling of the study. A massive, carved wooden desk with big round legs rested in front of a bay window.

This was the first time Lucy had been allowed into the room and she was excited. There would be more than enough books to last her an entire lifetime of reading.

"Hello," she said upon entering.

"It's about time, I've been waitin' hours," complained Oliver. He was stretched out on the floor playing a game with some polished stones.

Eugene was sitting in one of the comfy velvet chairs in the center of the room with his head in a book. He glanced up with a perturbed look on his face and pulled out his new pocket watch.

"Oliver, it's only half past eleven!" he informed his brother.

"Well, felt like hours!" countered Oliver.

Lucy paced the bookshelves, fingering the bindings as she scanned the titles.

"Yeh'll not find anythin' on bugs, I'm afraid," offered Eugene, stuffing the watch back inside his vest pocket.

"Actually, the one that interests me is not about insects," Lucy said, passing behind Eugene's chair.

Oliver jumped up and tugged at the purse that hung around her waist. He remembered he hadn't seen any of her drawings yet. After all, Lucy had promised him a peek only yesterday. "The drawin'. Can I have a look now?"

"Hang on," she waved him away. "All in due time."

Lucy spotted the book that she was looking for. Unfortunately, it was on the top shelf and just beyond her reach. She rose up on the tips of her toes, hoping to get the book, but it was of no use. She lost her balance and fell into the back of Eugene's chair, bumping his head along the way.

"Lucy Tuppins!" he howled bitterly. "This is a study, a place fer peace and quiet!"

"I didn't do it on purpose," scowled Lucy, pulling herself off the floor. "Sorry, Eugene."

"All right, which one did yeh want?" the older boy asked impatiently.

Lucy pointed to the brown book which was tucked between two black volumes, entitled *Book of English History & Nobility.*

Eugene struggled to get it down safely and placed it on his father's desk. "Couldn't yeh have selected a smaller book," he complained before returning to the comfy chair.

Lucy opened the book and slowly turned page by page. "Well, you see," she began, "I was wondering if there were any sketches in this reference."

"Don' think there are bugs in these books," her friend said, puzzled.

Lucy stopped and put her hand gently over Oliver's and stared directly into his eyes.

"Oliver," she whispered.

"Aye?" he whispered back.

"Can you keep a secret?"

Eugene burst out with laughter when he overheard them scheming. "Fat chance!" he remarked before burying his face back into his book.

It was then that Lucy decided to show Oliver one of her trinkets. She removed the coin from her purse and laid it on the desk.

"Blimey!" he hollered out. "What have yeh got there?"

Lucy put her finger to her lips. "Shush. You must promise not to tell anyone."

But Lucy realized too late that she had made the wrong decision in telling Oliver. Judging by his excitement he would definitely blabber out the fact that she had found a coin. And if her father knew, he'd take it from her.

"Eugene, it's gold!" shouted Oliver, hopping and pointing. "Come see!"

Eugene was annoyed by the interruption, but also curious about what Lucy was trying to hide. He put his book down and come over to investigate.

"Wherever did yeh get THAT?" he exclaimed in surprise, rubbing his eyes to make sure he wasn't seeing things.

Lucy leaned forward, and whispered conspiratorially, "I found it."

"It looks valuable," Eugene observed.

"I'm hoping there will be a sketch of it in this book," Lucy explained, turning the pages once again.

"Yeh're lookin' in the wrong place then," Eugene said, taking over the book and turning to the pages at the back. "There, I thought I'd seen sketches of old currency."

"Probably worth a bloody fortune," Oliver mused, picking up the gold piece and flipping it back and forth. "Just look how big it is!"

"There it is," declared Eugene, pointing to an image identical to what Oliver held in his hand.

"The Queen's holdings," breathed Lucy, "I can't believe it."

"Yeh know Lucy, this isn' somethin' yeh just find," Eugene said getting suspicious. He drilled Lucy for more information. "Tell me, who gave it ter yeh?"

"I told you already, I FOUND IT," Lucy raised her voice stubbornly.

"Says there that the coin was especially designed in 1800, and is part of England's royal treasury," read Eugene.

"Yeh mean ter tell me there are more of these?" asked Oliver, holding the coin up between them.

"Well, probably back in England," Eugene replied.

"What if I told you that this coin was right here on Maui?" Lucy asked. She grabbed the coin from Oliver and clenched it in her hand when she heard footsteps in the hall. "Remember when we were in the forest and you couldn't find me?"

"Playin' hide and seek, yeh were," explained Oliver.

"No, she wasn'," corrected Eugene with a smile. "She was lost."

Lucy sighed and shook her head. "You are both wrong. I was being detained. Burles came out of nowhere and grabbed me by the shoulder on the path." She continued to tell them about the first time she meet Burles on the ship in the dark corridor and she had found a coin.

"Whew!" said Oliver, "That one stinks."

"Okay, I'm confused," admitted Eugene. "Yeh found a coin out in the jungle?"

Lucy nodded. "I did."

"But he took it from you on the ship?" repeated Eugene, puzzled.

"No," she said, placing the coin on the image in the book. "That one is right here in front of us. He tried to take it, but I outwitted him now it is mine."

Oliver loved this kind of excitement and couldn't stand still. He leaped up and punched the air in delight. "That's our Lucy. Fought the big brute off."

"Thanks for the admiration, Oliver," said Lucy, sliding back into a chair with a grin.

"I must say, I'm havin' a bit of trouble following all this myself," confessed Eugene, scratching his head. "Think we better keep all this hush hush from mam until we find out more."

"I can keep a secret," assured Oliver.

"You really have to this time," insisted Lucy in a worried voice. "We don't know anything about this man. He could be capable of horrible things."

"Worse yet, Burles could be a criminal," added Eugene.

Oliver crinkled up his nose. "And he stinks of cigars. That should be a crime in itself!"

Silence settled on the trio as each one tried to figure out the mystery behind the coin. Something was definitely going on, and it probably needed investigating.

"The Queen was robbed, remember?" Lucy started in.

"Could have been him," suggested Eugene.

"Yes, it is possible. And he had to get away from England fast," Lucy continued their line of thought.

"With yehr ship sailin' the next day," pointed out Eugene, "it was the perfect escape. He's probably hidden the treasure on the island."

Oliver was feeling left out and kicked the game stones across the floor. "I think we should tell father."

"No!" Lucy and Eugene cried in unison. Oliver flinched at their outburst.

"I think that since I'm the oldest, I should hold onto the coin," Eugene reasoned.

Lucy put the coin back into her purse. She didn't fully trust Eugene and she wasn't going to risk losing her coin. "I don't think so. It stays right here with me," she said, patting her purse.

Lucy wasn't sure if Oliver would keep his mouth shut, so she decided to make him take an oath of secrecy. "Cross your heart, hope to die?"

"Never, never tell a lie," he finished the pact words and sealed it was the mark of a cross down his chest. "Yeh can count on me," he promised.

Seventeen

THE MISSION SCHOOL

A week had passed since Lucy first arrived on the island. Each day she discovered something new. And there was something mysterious about finding a gold coin and a gem. She was determined to find out where they came from. But that would have to wait till later.

Today, she was going to carry out a very important class assignment.

She stood on the *lanai* waiting for Elizabeth. It was her teacher who had come up with an interesting assignment to keep Lucy from being bored. Since Lucy loved science, Elizabeth outlined a project with scientific merit that perfectly suited her new little student.

Lucy was so excited to be getting the chance to observe Mrs. McBeal's classroom that she paced back and forth impatiently, clenching her notebook tightly against her chest.

The assignment was to document comparisons between the mission school and her class back in her home town of Ebley. She had to analyze her data and then come up with a theory.

Eugene and Oliver thought the entire assignment was just rubbish and a waste of time. But for Lucy, she welcomed the challenge.

Elizabeth finally came out the front door.

"Hurry up," Lucy pleaded, grabbing her teacher by the sleeve. "We're going to be late!"

The two of them started down the path to the village. They hadn't gotten far when they were approached by Reverend Machesney.

"Hey, wait up!" he called out, his flaming red hair bouncing in the morning breeze as he caught up with them. "I'll escort yeh."

"Oh, I'm sorry," said Elizabeth with a slight smile, "Lucy and I have ter prepare fer her lesson, and I would prefer we walk alone." Elizabeth took Lucy's arm and continued on, pretending to have an important discussion. The clergyman stopped in his tracks, clearly irritated by the rejection.

"Is he still there?" asked Elizabeth after a couple of minutes. Lucy glanced over her shoulder and saw that he was gone.

"No."

Elizabeth set out a sigh of relief. "That man gives me the creeps," she confided in Lucy. "He seems ter be everywhere!"

Lucy chatted all the way to the mission school, peppering Elizabeth with questions. Eugene and Oliver had arrived earlier with their mother.

"Why is there a tree in the middle of the road?" Lucy asked.

"If yeh look close enough, yeh'll see that the *kuma*, I mean teachers, are showin' the young men how ter hollow out the wood," she replied.

"But why?" Lucy pressed on.

"They're makin' a boat," Oliver joined in, pointing across the center of the village. He and Eugene spotted them when they entered the clearing and came to greet them. "It's goin' ter be an outrigger canoe like the ones that are all polished over there," he continued, pointing to the shiny long boats.

Then someone caught Oliver's eye. It was Kalani. Although Reverend McBeal forbid Oliver from playing with the island boys, the young lad seemed to manage plenty of opportunities to sneak off and do just that. He tugged repeatedly at Elizabeth's sleeve until her waist buttons started popping open. "Can I go over there? Can I? Can I?" the eager boy pestered his sister.

Elizabeth yanked her arm away. "Now see what yeh've done!" Embarrassed, she quickly refastened her skirt. "Oh, all right. Yeh can go. But first Eugene has ter take Lucy over ter the school before she's late. I'm goin' ter join the old *wahine*. We need some vegetables fer dinner. Meet up with yeh in an hour, over by the cookin' pits."

The children watched Elizabeth strut across the clearing in the opposite direction from the school.

"Vegetables! Right!" Eugene said sarcastically.

"Is Elizabeth going to meet up with Kalani, too," asked Lucy.

"Sure, he's her gentleman friend," offered Oliver.

"Great!," remarked Eugene, giving his brother a scathing look. "Yeh remember how Elizabeth said it's a secret ter keep close ter yehr heart? Now yeh've gone and done it, Oliver," he scolded.

"But I only told Lucy. Elizabeth wouldn' mind, really she won'," Oliver said, trying to defend himself for betraying Elizabeth's trust.

"That's not the point. If our father ever finds out that Elizabeth fancies Kalani, there will be awful trouble," Eugene lectured his brother.

"Why is that?" asked Lucy.

"We're not supposed ter mix with their kind," Eugene stated.

"Mix? Mix what?" she asked, not understanding what the problem was.

The older boy shrugged. "Huggin', kissin', all that sort of thin', I suppose."

Oliver scrunched up his face. "Yuck!" He turned and ran across the road to the wood carvers.

When Lucy and her escort turned the corner and saw the school, the little girl grabbed ahold of Eugene's hand and murmured, "Eugene, your mum's school is fantastic."

"It isn't that great," Eugene said, shaking off Lucy's hand. "They don' even have any books. But that will all change when Mr. Loomis arrives with a printin' press."

Lucy stepped up onto the *lanai*. "I don't see why I can't come to this school."

"English, mathematics, history, proper writing, and reading studies. They don' learn any of that here! Now do yeh understand?" he explained in that condescending tone Lucy had grown to detest.

"Are yeh quite finished, Eugene?" asked Mrs. McBeal, coming to lean over the railing behind her son. "Be a good lad now and come here. I need yehr help."

"Honestly Mam, now?"

"Now," she replied firmly. To her guest for the school day, Mrs. McBeal spoke more kindly, "Lucy, yeh can go ahead and explore the village. I'll ring the bell when it's time ter come back."

Lucy strolled down the small path where huts of *pili* grass and bamboo branches lined the center of the village. No one had left her alone since she arrived and she was very pleased to be able to freely wander about on her own.

She looked around and noticed that there were only elders and young women. *That's strange. Where are all the men?*, she thought. The gray haired old men sat in front of their huts staring at the little blonde girl from across the sea. But there was one old man who ignored her.

She noticed him because he sat all alone on a mat surrounded by piles of green leaves. She watched as he slowly took his large brown hands and pressed down into the foliage.

He was so busy with his task that he didn't notice when Lucy approached.

"Hello there!" greeted Lucy. "My name is Lucy; Lucy Tuppins," she introduced herself, trying to get his attention. But he never returned her greeting and went on with whatever he was doing. Lucy watched him with curiosity and wondered why his teeth didn't ache when he placed a large flat *ti* leaf into his mouth, bit it at the spine, and pulled the back bone off with his front teeth. *Astonishing,* she thought.

He was dressed in a swatch of *tapa* fabric tied around his waist. It didn't cover much of his dark skin. Lucy wondered if it was part of a costume because he didn't look like the rest of the elders. His dark hair was pulled tight against his scalp and twisted into a topknot. All the other men had long, wavy gray hair and wore long fabrics around their waists.

"He doesn't speak English very well," offered a young island girl, who looked about fourteen years old. She had appeared in the opening in the old man's hut and was the prettiest girl Lucy had seen in the village. Her black, waist-length hair swayed in the slight breeze as she walked over and sat down next to the old man and shared a few hushed words.

"This is my grandfather," she continued. "The people of the village call him *Hoku*. He wants you to sit here."

The old man patted a pile of leaves for Lucy. The ground was still hard to Lucy's backside, but she didn't mind. Then she watched as he leaned forward and placed a *lei* of leaves around her neck.

"*O mai o Hoku, aloha,*" he said.

"It is a *maile lei* that he gives you. Very special and given on great occasions," explained the girl.

"Fanatastic," exclaimed Lucy, smelling the sweet leaves. She extended her hand to the older girl, "I'm Lucy. Pleased to meet you."

The girl pushed the hand away and told Lucy that it was not their custom to shake hands. Instead, she leaned forward and touched Lucy's nose with her own.

"I'm Maile," the pretty island girl offered.

"Maile! Like the leaf?" Lucy replied happily.

"Yes," the girl smiled back.

"*Mai ka moemoea mai 'oia,*" spoke *Hoku.*

"He says that you are the one from the dreams," translated Maile.

"He's been dreaming about me, too?" Lucy asked in surprise.

She listened to Maile relate the story about the Chief and his prophetic dream. Every islander thought that she would bring great good to their land. But Lucy dismissed the notion, saying, "I doubt that it was me, I'm only eight." She averted her eyes from *Hoku* because he was making her feel uneasy.

"What are these for?" she said, changing the subject and looking down at the various bowls of crushed leaves and berries.

"Grandfather is our *kahuna lapa-au*, a healer," Maile informed her.

"Oh, a doctor," the little girl replied.

"He's had many visions that help our people. His power is very strong. All come to him for healing."

Suddenly the old man reached over and placed his large hand on Lucy's purse. He looked straight into her eyes and frowned.

"What is it?" she asked him.

Maile explained that her grandfather wanted to give Lucy a warning about the contents of the purse.

"I have a coin, that's all," claimed Lucy.

"*Keiki*, it brings evil with it," cautioned the old man.

"No, it doesn't," she argued, slipping it into the palm of her hand. "See? It's just a coin."

"Lucy, be careful," counseled Maile.

Hoku placed a hand on each of the little girl's shoulders.

"He can feel your *uhane*, spirit, Lucy," said Maile in a soft voice. "It's the shield that surrounds you and protects you from harm."

"If I had a shield, I think I would know it," she said. Lucy slouched down and slid out from under the old man's grip, getting wary.

"But you do. Please listen to what he has to say," pleaded Maile.

Lucy had heard enough about herself, but thought maybe this old man could tell her more about the mysterious little people in the forest Oliver kept mentioning.

"Maybe it will protect me from the *Menehune*. What do you think?" she asked, carefully changing the subject.

"How do you know of the *Menehune*?" mumbled *Hoku*, staring at her with wide eyes.

"Oliver told me," replied Lucy, perking up at his attentive reaction.

"There are little people where I come from, too. They're called Leprechauns, and we talk about them all the time," said Lucy.

"*Mahope aku e wahawale ana 'oia no Menhune?*" asked *Hoku.*

Maile, continuing to translate her grandfather's Hawaiian words said, "Lucy Tuppins. What I'm going to tell you, you must hold deep inside of you. What you call a secret. Grandfather says that you will know of the small people in due time. But you must understand that they are very precious to us. We protect them."

"Then it's true," the little girl said eagerly. "Not just one of Oliver's made up tales?"

Lucy was very excited and assured Maile that she would keep the secret. After all, she was keeping a few secrets at that very moment. One more wouldn't be too much to ask of her.

Maile took a deep breath and told Lucy the first story of the *Menehune.* She spoke of a tribe of small people, something like the gnomes found in English fairy tales, who left their land of Mu by canoe and made the long journey across the ocean to the island.

Lucy looked about the village to see if she could recognize any of the little people, but there were only tall islanders around.

Maile continued her telling, and recalled old tales that told of the great Polynesian chiefs who protected the *Menehune.* And in return for that kindness, the small people dug wells, cleared forests, and built walls, roads, and bridges. They were the architects and engineers of the islands.

"I don't see them," said Lucy, fidgeting on the pile of slippery leaves.

"That's because they hide," explained Maile. "Through the years, foreigners have treated them badly – taken them, and made them work very hard. Like the slaves in Egypt."

"Don't they ever come into the village?" asked Lucy.

"There are scores of them on this island. But they only work at night when everyone is asleep."

Lucy stood up then. She liked a good story, but this one sounded like another fairy tale to her. So, she smiled politely and turned to leave without saying anything.

"Wait," Maile called after her. "Grandfather holds the knowledge. It is only through him that they reveal themselves. He says that you have the same knowledge, Lucy. You must keep it deep down. We must protect the *Menehune*." The island girl was desperate to convince Lucy to keep the *Menehune* a secret and tried to stop her by grabbing her sleeve.

Seconds later they were interrupted by the arrival of Eugene. Lucy looked up when she heard the school bell ringing.

"Hello, Maile," greeted Eugene, bowing. "Got any good stories today?" he continued with a slight smile.

"Aloha e, Eugene," Maile responded, smiling graciously.

"English, remember?" Eugene corrected her. To Lucy, he said, "Maile is one of Mam's best pupils. She just graduated from the first mission school class."

"She's very good," admitted Lucy.

"Lucy, we've got ter go," said Eugene.

Lucy turned to Maile and smiled. "Goodbye, Maile and thank you for the story."

"It was a pleasure making your acquaintance, Miss Lucy," Maile returned.

As Lucy and Eugene walked toward the school, she turned and waved to *Hoku*.

"Better not believe everythin' the islanders tell yeh. Superstitions and stories, that's all they are," advised Eugene.

Eighteen

Lucinda's Locket

August, 1826

Two months ago, Lucy arrived on the island in the heart of summer. Now the smells of summer filled the air with rotting vegetation and dead fish odors down at the beach. The rains had finally stopped and it was sweltering hot. But everyone welcomed the cool breezes flowing down from the mountain top and blanketing the village in the late evening hours.

Lucy's father worked very hard to get his new church built. And after months of agonizing heat and construction, today was the day everyone across the island would come to hear his first sermon in the new church.

But Lucy didn't have to go to a fancy church to talk to God. She talked to Him all the time. Every morning, the very first thing she'd do even before getting out of bed was to say, "Good morning." Then she'd start talking about anything that was in her thoughts. Things like: "Thank you God for stopping the rain," and "Please watch over my Papa, today."

This morning was starting the same way until Lucy heard the snapping of a branch outside her bedroom window. She quickly went over to the sill and saw Oliver stretched out and dozing on a large branch.

"Oliver!" she whispered. "You weren't out there all night, were you?"

"Of course not, lassie," he replied drowsily.

Lucy climbed out over her windowsill and easily maneuvered the twists and turns in the branches, making her way over to her climbing buddy.

"What are you doing?" she asked.

"Do I have ter be doin' anythin'?" he asked back.

"I guess not," she replied after quick consideration.

Lucy stretched out alongside Oliver and looked up through the tree. She saw three birds' nests and watched as the green and yellow finches fluttered back and forth feeding their babies.

"I wish I could just stay in this tree all day," sighed Oliver.

"No, you don't," remarked Lucy.

"Aye, that I do," he countered. "This is what a Sunday is supposed ter be like. The Lord commanded it."

"Oliver," said Lucy, "you've got it mixed up a bit. There is to be no work. He didn't say anything about skipping church service."

Just then Mrs. McBeal's voice sounded throughout the house. She was announcing breakfast, and Lucy knew that she was going to be in trouble. She wasn't even dressed yet.

"Blasts," she said, crawling across a limb towards her window. "I'll see you later, Oliver."

Lucy swung open the wooden wardrobe in her room, releasing the scent of sweet lavender into the air. She snatched a dress off its hanger. It was a special dress that she had saved for this very Sunday morning.

She rubbed the smooth, soft satin against her cheek. Her nana had sewn it for her with love. It didn't take Lucy long to shed the nightgown and slip into the delicate lace pinafore. But as the cloth slid down her slim body, something scratched her shoulder.

"Ouch!" she cried out with a jump.

She sat down on her bed and carefully ran her fingers along the row of tiny periwinkle flowers that were crocheted along the seam, examining the hemline for the hard object. When she came upon a bulge in the fabric, Lucy worked it back and forth until it popped out around the thread.

To her surprise, it was a locket. She'd seen it before, but couldn't remember where. How did it wind up in her dress?

The tiny silver lid easily lifted and Lucy found a small note tucked inside. Heart racing with excitement, she quickly unfolded the paper and saw from the handwriting that it was from her nana. She read it aloud:

Your mother was a brave lady, little Lucy. She fought to stay in this life with you. Now it is up to you to be brave. Deep down you possess the strength of the Lucindas, and when you are lost in that place of darkness and doubt, hold the locket. It will fill you with hope.

Lucy's eyes pooled with tears. Then she saw the image of her mother and a strand of blonde hair nestled under a piece of glass on the inside of the silver lid. She touched it with a kiss. "Mum, I miss you," Lucy whispered.

As she held the locket, memories flooded back to her. She remembered visiting her grandmother when she was very young. The old lady lived in a forest not far from Ebley. She also remembered that the locket once hung from a chain around her nana's neck. Her nana would tell her stories about the Lucindas in the family, but she was so young that she'd forgotten them. Lucy wondered how many Lucindas had worn this very locket before her. She slipped the chain around her neck and tucked it safely under the dress.

There was one thing however, that she did remember clearly. And that was the fact that her father disliked her nana. He would not have approved of the locket, so Lucy would need to keep it hidden for now.

The little girl was glancing around the room one more time before heading downstairs when she noticed her purse. It was dangling from the bedpost. Lucy knew that if she put it around her waist, the dirt would rub off and spoil her new dress. After a moment of thinking, she decided to hide it away in her room while she was away at church.

Finding a good hiding spot was hard. But she finally found the perfect location. Her mattress was stuffed with *kiawe* beans. She poked a hole in the seam where she tucked away the gem and coin.

In the hallway of the white house Lucy bumped into Reverend Machesney. She was surprised to see him and at first just stared blankly at him wondering why he was wandering around upstairs, since his room was outside over the horse stable.

"Oh, sorry," she apologized, curtsying and feeling glad that she had hidden her trinkets. The big man was always turning up, especially around Elizabeth, and it annoyed Lucy.

"Lucy, is that you?" called out the Bishop from the lanai. "Hurry up."

She was quite relieved that her father had summoned her at that very moment. She glanced at the Reverend, smiled, and ran down the staircase exiting out the front door and not looking back for a second.

Just beyond the tree line Lucy could see the metal church steeple glistening brightly in the morning sunshine.

She didn't understand why her father had ordered the trees cut down. There once was a fine forest which separated the *taro* field and settlement from the house. Now just a line of stray gangling gigantic tree trunks stood there, swaying in the cool morning breeze.

Lucy feared that the *taro* would suffer the same fate as the trees if they were in the way of her father's building project.

She knew from Maile how important the forest and the *taro* patches were for the islanders' survival. The thought of the *taro* disappearing forever made her very sad.

"And how is my princess this fine day?" greeted her father.

"Good morning, Papa," Lucy greeted him. "You seem very happy today. I overheard a bit of your sermon last night and I think it sounds fantastic. How many people will be coming today?"

"If they have a good mind to be saved and enter the Lord's pearly gates," he stated, "then the entire island should be there." He turned his head at the sound of a jingling buggy bell. "Ah, there's Reverend McBeal with our ride!"

Lucy jumped up and down, waving as Oliver's father approached. There was no mistaking the similarity in the fuzzy mop hair that swayed on their heads. She was excited to be able to ride to church in his polished black cart.

"Top of the mornin' to yeh," announced the Reverend, tipping his hat when he stopped in front of the house. "Yeh're lookin' quite lovely today, Miss Lucy."

"Do you think so?" she said with a smile, twirling in her new dress.

"Is there still time for you to come in for a spot of breakfast?" the Bishop asked.

"Certainly not!" declared the Reverend, patting the seat next to him. "We'd best be off now. The *lau hala* mats are all laid out on the floor and the children and women are already arrivin' at the church. There's no time ter waste."

Nineteen

Net Fishing

Not everyone on the island came to hear the Bishop's sermon that morning because of the excitement on the beach. Hundreds of young island men from across the island had come to catch fish swirling in the bay.

"*Aloha e*, old healer," called Kalani, tying up his fishing net and securing the heavy ropes.

He was glad to see that his friend *Hoku* had come to watch them catch the *o'pelu*. It was to be the first catch of the season and the fish had swarmed into the bay, swimming in a frenzied ball.

Maile had come too. She helped her grandfather over the rocks along the shoreline to where Kalani was. But she was a little more interested in getting a good look at the boys than the fishing.

"*Aloha*," greeted *Hoku*, poking Kalani with his walking stick.

"Come to bless our catch?" asked Kalani. "Too late, we have already caught plenty of fish to feed the entire village for weeks. The gods have been good to us this day."

"Fish come for today. It is good," pronounced the old man. "Work hard."

"Ah," said Kalani, pulling at the ropes again, "you're speaking English. Good."

"Practicing," Hoku admitted.

Maile casually asked Kalani if his nets were good. She liked him very much but all the young girls on the island knew that he'd given his heart to Elizabeth.

Kalani knew and respected their feelings, but he could only be their friend. "Everyone is here," he continued talking with Maile. "The sound of the shell brought Kimo from Polipoli and Kekoa from Kanaio. Look, over there." Kalani pointed to his friends on the beach.

"Oh yes, I see," she replied. The distances between the villages sometimes seemed like huge walls to the island teenagers, and Maile knew that soon every girl in her village would be on the beach to check out the visiting boys. There would be fierce competition to nab the best ones, so to get a head start she released her hair from the bun on top of her head. Maile hoped to catch some of the boys' eyes as her silky brown strands flowed in the soft wind.

They were intent on their task though; and the boys all marched into the water together, holding long nets high above their heads. Then all of a sudden everyone stopped.

An unfamiliar sound rang through the valleys and across the beach, piercing the air with a hard clank of metal striking metal. The noise bounced off the cliff walls. Frightened birds flew out of their treetop roosts and filled the sky.

Kalani turned to *Hoku*. "What is it?" he asked.

The old man explained that the large bell on the new church was ringing, and the Bishop's sermon would begin shortly.

"Go!" Kalani shouted to his friends, pointing further out into the ocean, "It doesn't concern us." He knew that they were there today to net the biggest catch of the season, and nothing was going to stop them.

"We have to leave now," Maile excused herself and her grandfather. Kalani nodded and turned to join his friends in the water. She helped the old man back to the firm footing of the forest path. "Grandfather," she asked, "the new church, it is good, yes?"

But *Hoku* didn't answer. He sensed there was danger up ahead. "Hurry," he ordered, pulling her arm in another direction.

"What is wrong?" Maile inquired.

"We must go another way," he replied.

Hidden in the forest, a man lurked behind a clump of bushes. He was watching the young men, and was impressed by the way they lifted the heavy nets, demonstrating great strength and power. Burles knew that he needed more workers to finish building the mission settlement, and he began concocting a plan to recruit these islanders into his workforce.

Twenty

THE SERMON

There were so many gods worshiped by the islanders that Lucy had a hard time remembering which one did what. Pele was a very popular god that Lucy heard mentioned the moment the weather turned bad. Pele was considered the goddess of the volcanos. Lucy learned from Maile that the islanders considered Kane to be their creator but then there was Mokualii, the god of the canoe makers; Kuula, the god of fishermen; and Kanoloa, the god of the ocean. *All these gods is so confusing. Wouldn't it be much easier just having one god in charge of everything?*, she thought. She always believed that her God was the creator of the heavens and the earth. Her nana would tell her that meant she had faith. "What's that?" she once asked her grandmother. "Faith is a powerful thing that comes from the deepest part of your soul," she told Lucy.

"It's the bond of love and trust with your Creator that can never be broken."

Lucy gazed around the new church at all the islanders listening to her father, who was perched high up in a wooden pulpit. He gripped the sides of the platform as he hurled down his powerful damnation sermon.

"He's makin' the wee ones cry," murmured Oliver, nudging Lucy's side.

"Shush," she replied.

"But they aren't goin' ter like God if yehr father scares them ter death," hissed Oliver.

There weren't any wooden benches or seats in the church yet. Everyone sat on *lau hala* mats that were woven from palm branches just for this new building.

Lucy sat with the McBeal family in the front row while hundreds of islanders gathered on the other mats. Bishop Tuppins was excited that the most prominent person on the island was one of the attendees.

"I don't see why he gets to be right up on the altar," muttered Lucy, looking at the Chief sitting on the raised platform. "It just isn't right."

"He has ter be higher than everyone else, Lucy," explained Oliver. "He's like a god ter his people."

Lucy sighed. She'd listened to her father tell people of God, but he never claimed to be a god himself. She hoped that the Chief didn't think he was equal to God, because that just wouldn't be right.

Her father continued talking and talking.

"God condemned Adam and Eve to a life of suffering, toil, and hardships. It was because of their disobedience, YES," he shouted, and even Lucy jumped when he banged his palm on the pulpit. "I say it is through disobedience that you continue to atone for that sin."

Lucy wondered if the little chocolate colored kids even knew what sin was. They always looked so innocent, and she'd never heard of any of them doing anything wrong.

Suddenly, her father stopped speaking. Everyone turned around and stared at *Hoku* making his entrance from the back of the building. No one even dared to cough in the silence until the old healer found his place among the women and children.

Bishop Tuppins breathed out a deep sigh and continued his talk.

"Embrace, yes, embrace that burden. For it separates us from nonbelievers," said her father, turning to his side and looking right at the Chief. "Those that have not been saved by God will never, I said NEVER -," he slammed down the bible on the wooden surface and once again everyone jumped up in fright.

"There he goes again," remarked Oliver, giggling this time.

"Stop that, Oliver," whispered Lucy.

"- enter the kingdom of heaven. So, in the name of the church, I ask of you," stressed the Bishop, leaning closer toward the islanders, "Obey God's commandments. It is through hard work and suffering that He will know your atonement is genuine." As he finished, he looked over at Mrs. McBeal, who was seated at the pump organ.

"There it is," whispered Oliver, "work. And what's this about sufferin'? Nope, I don' like his message at all."

Before Lucy could respond, Reverend McBeal stood and led everyone in a selection of hymns. Lucy thought Mrs. McBeal looked very silly playing the instrument, her legs floating up and down under her black linen skirt as she pumped air into the organ's pipes.

After the church service, Bishop Tuppins greeted the Chief and his followers at the front door. Lucy was at his side.

"Fine day, Bishop Tuppins," said the Chief, surrounded by his many wives.

"Our gratitude for your kindness, Your Highness," the Bishop bowed before his honored guest and thanked him for coming.

Lucy didn't like having to stand next to her father. She thought, i*t just wasn't fair that Oliver got to go off and play while she had to stand there curtsying to each and every person who attended the service. It would be lunchtime before she finished curtsying to them all!*

"Stand up straight, Lucy," ordered the Bishop nudging his daughter's lower back.

"Yes, I'm pleased with the building," continued the Chief in a deep voice. "Should please your god."

The Bishop continued to talk with the Chief while Lucy stood there, growing increasingly bored. She reached out and touched one of the women's bright blue silk scarves as it floated up in the air. "Fantastic," she said, admiring the feel of the soft fabric.

"Lucy!" her father cried out. "Mind your manners."

But the Chief only smiled in amusement. "Ah, little *keiki*. Yes, you like it? A gift from Burles to all my *wahine*."

She felt the pressure of her father's hand on her shoulder. She knew that it was a sign that she was in trouble, or soon to be in trouble for interrupting their talk.

"Bishop Tuppins," resumed the Chief, "I hear you are a good businessman."

"If you mean the business of the Lord, well, then I believe I am guilty," admitted the Bishop.

"This settlement of yours, it will be good for my people. True?" posed the ruler.

Bishop Tuppins answered readily, "It is true. There are many souls here that will benefit."

"Then you will have your land cleared, your bridges made, and your buildings built soon. I command it," the Chief nodded with satisfaction.

"Thank you, Your Highness," said the Bishop, grinning from ear to ear.

But there was no grin on Lucy's face. The Chief's words made something knot up in her stomach. Maybe she was sick and could go home now instead of curtsying more. But Mrs. McBeal had other plans and pulled Lucy to the side.

121

"Where are you taking me?" the little girl asked.

"The Lord's work is never done," stated Mrs. McBeal, leading Lucy by the hand back into the church and to the pulpit, where Oliver and Eugene were already waiting.

"What's going on?" Lucy whispered to them. She watched Mrs. McBeal stand next to Reverend Machesney and Reverend McBeal by the altar. With a swift pull of her arm, she swung a large red velvet curtain closed, concealing the three adults behind it. The children were now alone in the church.

"That's our cue," said Eugene. "Here, roll these up." He handed Lucy a floor mat.

Oliver climbed up into the pulpit. It was built on a platform so that the Bishop could look down at the people. But Lucy thought that maybe it was built higher so her father could be closer to God.

Oliver stood up on the tips of his toes and looked over the podium with the stoic expression of a preacher. He loudly cleared his throat and called out, "And furthermore, I plead with each and every one of you -." He stopped abruptly when Eugene tossed a rag at him and whispered, "Shush!"

Lucy and Oliver hadn't noticed when Reverend Machesney came to stand outside the curtain. "Are yeh quite finished, Oliver?" he demanded, with his hands on his hips.

"Leave him alone," demanded Eugene, moving toward his brother. "He's just a kid."

Oliver hurried down from the pulpit and stood by Lucy and Eugene.

"If yeh were mine, there'd be a punishment fer that mockery," threatened the Reverend as he came close.

"Well, thank the good Lord that we aren't yours!" retorted Lucy, stepping in front of Oliver. She crossed her arms against her chest, facing the Reverend in a defensive position.

Reverend Machesney glared furiously at Lucy. He was about to grab her by the shoulders when Bishop Tuppins finally concluded his greetings outside the church and re-entered through the front doors. At that same moment, Mrs. McBeal and the Reverend McBeal came out from behind the curtain.

Lucy had been confident that she could outwit Reverend Machesney, but she was very glad to see her father just then coming over to the altar. He was muttering something to himself and seemed to ignore the presence of the children.

"No, no," the Bishop continued, "these heathens will never understand the importance of diligence and discipline." He stood in front of the McBeals shaking his head.

Oliver piped up, "Aye, but I think yeh scared them, sir."

Once again the Bishop appeared to ignore the children and continued, "Fishing. Ha! Most of them were down at the ocean fishing, and on a Sunday, no less."

"Yeh can't blame them fer it," put in Reverend McBeal.

"Stop coddling them," the Bishop said angrily.

"But Bishop," pleaded Mrs. McBeal. "It was the first catch of the season. Surely, yeh want them ter be able ter feed their children?"

"Don't they know that I want them all to be saved; men, women, and children alike?" continued the Bishop, paying her no mind. "I can't believe just the women and children came."

"Two years and we've come so far with them," reassured Mrs. McBeal. "Don' give up hope, now."

"But not far enough," emphasized the Bishop. "They're just being lazy. Now is the time to push them. And the sooner the better, I say."

Lucy had never seen her father so riled up before. She knew that he was disappointed at the number who didn't show up to hear him speak, but she didn't understand what he meant by pushing the islanders, or why. And she didn't like the tone of his voice.

Twenty-One

Taro Patches

The day after the Bishop spoke of hard work and sacrifice, the Chief stood on the bluff overlooking the stream that fed the taro patches. He had ordered the islanders to cut down the *sandlewood* trees that grew for hundreds of years next to the running water.

Burles also stood on the bluff. He was pleased that the Chief had ordered all the young men to clear the land for the new bridges. But he was not happy about the fact that the Chief didn't want to tear up the *taro* patches.

"*Taro* stays there," said the island leader firmly, pointing to the patchwork of green-leafed plants that grew in the stream and fed his people. They had been planted by the first Polynesian settlers, hundreds of years before.

"Must I remind you again that you agreed to the plans?" asked Burles, rolling out the paper drawings. "Over there.

We will construct a series of bridges which will connect the east side of the settlement with the older village."

"There is no east or west," claimed the Chief. "*Taro* stays there!"

"I don't think you're listening, Chief," Burles attempted again. He swept his arm over the scene. "All of this is to be torn down to make way for the new irrigation system. No more *taro* down there. There will be farms, that's the plan."

Burles was a master of deceit and was used to eventually getting things his way. He continued trying to convince the Chief that the islanders would have a much better life with the new plan, he explainied that they wouldn't have to work in the 'filthy ditches' or spend their days toiling and slaving over the gigantic purple carrot they called *taro*.

"Farms with livestock, just think of it," urged Burles.

"Spirited water," said the Chief eagerly, looking into Burles face, "you still have much stored? How much?"

"Enough to make you happy for a long time," answered Burles with a smile. He knew the Chief would do just about anything for more liquor, and Burles had plenty of rum stashed away.

"My *wahine* want more silk. You have plenty more?"

Burles saw his chances. "Okay, Chief. You get the islanders to finish all the building before the next ship arrives, and I promise you will have all the silk and rum you want."

"Okay," agreed the Chief, nodding his head.

"It's a deal then," said Burles, quite pleased with himself. He had just managed to persuade the ruler of the island to let him destroy whatever he wanted – and all for some silk and rum.

The foreman left the Chief on the bluff to go survey the work being done. When he arrived further downstream, he saw a group of young men working to repair a retaining wall to save the *taro* patches from drying up.

"STOP!" Burles furiously shouted at them.

He didn't want the wall repaired because he planned to divert the water from the area into a pond. The streambed would dry up and the settlement's farm fields would get all the water. Burles ordered them to destroy the wall.

When the islanders refused, Burles reached inside his cape to pull out a whip and snapped it near them. The crack of the leather was so loud that it could be heard up the valley. He was giving them warning to do exactly as he instructed. But the workers didn't move and instead looked up to their Chief.

The Chief ignored their silent pleas, commanding them to pick up the boulders and destroy the wall. None of them moved. Then Burles' anger boiled over and he struck some of the young men with his whip.

The islanders became saddened when they saw their Chief did nothing to stop the cruelty of this man. So unwillingly, they formed a long line and pushed the boulders into the clearing, knowing it would destroy the *taro* patches.

The forest seemed to feel their sadness and everything hushed. The tree branches stilled, the fresh wind that blew strong died away, and even the sweet bird song that normally rippled through the leaves went silent. It was as if every living thing felt the evil that had come to the land.

Kalani was on the other side of the stream gathering branches in the *hala* forest when he heard the splintering noise of a whip cracking.

Alarmed, he dropped the bundle and ran along the forest path, until he came to the edge of the trees.

He couldn't believe what he saw before him. Kalani's eyes filled with tears as he gazed at the place where lush *taro* had once thrived, nourished by the sparkling water of a stream. Now the land was a horrifying expanse of death and dirt. The walls were gone and the stream emptied into the fallow clearing.

His beloved home was being destroyed.

"What is this madness?" he asked the men, crouching down between them as they pushed the boulders.

"Plans," replied one of the men. "Settlement plans."

"But without the water from the stream the *taro* will dry up and die. Nothing to eat," he whispered, watching Burles.

"Be careful," warned another man. "That one over there. He has much power."

"Not as much as my father," Kalani said with pride.

The man shielded Kalani close to his body. "But it is your father, the Chief, who ordered this work," he explained, pointing to the bluff.

Kalani's heart sank as he watched his father turn his back on their people. He was witnessing the destruction of the land. The land they called *'aina* that had defined their way of life for centuries was disappearing.

"And the trees, did he order them to be cut down as well?" Kalani asked.

A young man who bled from a whip-wound answered hopelessly, "Yes. Tomorrow we start work on the bridges."

Kalani couldn't believe it. He remembered that his father had once been a great warrior who defended their land from outsiders. But that was long ago, and Kalani didn't recognize the man on the slope anymore. He didn't want to believe that his father was willing to trade culture and beauty for liquor and silk.

Disappointed, Kalani turned away and snuck off into the village below, never looking back.

Twenty-Two

A Science Lesson

Burles' voice boomed through the air. When Lucy heard it, a chill ran down her spine.

Elizabeth was lecturing Eugene and Oliver on England's fine navel accomplishment when Lucy left the window and took her seat at the end of the long wooden table in the dining room.

She had finished her studies over an hour ago, and sketching was the only thing she could think of to get her mind off the distractions outside. The earth shook under the house as huge trees from the forest nearby crashed to the ground.

"That's it fer the day, class," announced Elizabeth. "Put away yehr thins'." She stood behind Lucy admiring the little girl's drawing of a Queen with a fat belly and dangling neck jewels.

"But Elizabeth," protested Eugene, looking down at his watch, "it's only half past ten!"

"Aye, and yeh're so diligent in yehr lessons that yeh feel the need fer more assignments, do yeh?" Elizabeth asked, raising an eyebrow.

"No," snapped Eugene, closing his notebook. "Yeh know that's not what I meant."

"I think it's grand that we're done early," remembered Oliver, running over to the window.

"Besides, I have plans fer Lucy," continued Elizabeth. "She will be presentin' her insect sketches ter mam's class today."

"Those old things?" muttered Eugene, wrinkling up his nose.

"At least someone respects my research," remarked Lucy, grinning from ear to ear.

"She's only eight! How can she teach a class?" retorted Eugene, purposely trying to annoy Lucy.

"Enough of yehr complainin'," said Elizabeth. She pointed towards the door to the hallway. "Eugene, yeh and Oliver go help Leah in the garden."

"What?" Eugene whined.

"Eugene, if I were you," Lucy said smugly, "I'd take this opportunity to learn all of the fine lessons of farming. You never know, maybe you'll find it's your calling."

Lucy knew all too well that Eugene didn't want to be a farmer. He would think it beneath his intelligence. Even though his family was settled down here in the Sandwich Islands, he had his sights set on going back to England to become a financial professional.

"Hardly," Eugene snapped, tugging to straighten the ends of his vest. "I'm a proper English gentleman. Going to be a banker, I am."

Lucy couldn't help giggling then. She was imagining him falling flat on his face from such a pompous attitude, his nose so far in the air that he couldn't see where he was going.

Oliver started laughing, too.

"Well," Elizabeth cut in, trying to regain order in the classroom. "Whatever yeh'll be in ten years can wait. Today yeh'll be helpin' Leah in the garden. And that's that!" She turned and gathered up her teaching things off the table

Lucy and Oliver's bellies were hurting so badly from laughter that they had to bend forward and take deep breaths.

Eugene leaned into Lucy, "I can hold onto the coin, for safe keepin' that is. Yeh won't want my mam ter see it in yehr box," Eugene whispered.

"I have it tucked in a safe place already, thank you very much," Lucy whispered back.

A moment later, Elizabeth was towering over the two conspirators. In a rather loud voice, she startled them and asked, "What are yeh two gossipin' about?"

Lucy straightened up, defensively. "You scared the living daylights out of me!" she exclaimed.

As the boys headed for the door, Eugene thought of something and turned back to Lucy. "Keep yehr ears open," he advised in a low tone. "Yeh might hear somethin' in the village about yeh-know-what."

"Off with the two of yeh," ordered Elizabeth, waving her arms at her brothers. "Into the garden with Leah, now."

The coin had remained hidden in Lucy's mattress since yesterday. However, she didn't feel it was safe to leave it there today while she journeyed into the village. Her feet scampered up to the top of the stairs. She retrieved her purse with its coin inside and was about to head back downstairs when she heard Reverend Machesney's voice below.

"Good day, Miss Elizabeth."

"Good day, Reverend," her teacher responded politely.

"A fine one, too. I understand that yeh will be goin' into the village today. It would be a great honor ter accompany yeh," said the Reverend.

"That won' be necessary," Elizabeth declined.

"Probably not necessary, but a beautiful lady such as yehrself shouldn' be travelin' unaccompanied," persisted the young clergyman.

Lucy looked down over the railing and saw Elizabeth standing with her back against the wall. The Reverend had Elizabeth cornered. He must have been watching and waiting for a chance to get Elizabeth alone again.

"What is the meanin 'of this?" demanded Elizabeth's father exiting the kitchen just then. He took the young clergyman by the arm and pushed him to the front door.

"I was just offerin' – ," began Reverend Machesney.

"I don' care what yeh were offerin'. This is my daughter and I never want ter see yeh closer than five feet from her.

Do yeh understand?" Reverend McBeal twisted the young clergyman's arm, still fuming.

"Aye, sir," Reverend Machesney winced.

When Elizabeth's father released his grip, the young clergyman stormed out of the door. Lucy had never seen Reverend McBeal stir with such a temper.

"Are yeh alright?" he asked his daughter.

"Of course, father. Thank you. I think he has feelin's fer me, but I can't stand him," Elizabeth admitted. Reverend McBeal nodded in agreement.

Elizabeth caught a glimpse of Lucy standing at the top of the staircase. She was relieved to see the little girl because her father was about to launch into one of his drawn out speeches about manners.

"Oh, Lucy!" said Elizabeth. "Father, please excuse me. Lucy and I best be goin', or we'll be late fer the lesson."

When Lucy and Elizabeth arrived at the mission school, they were greeted by a class of excited children.

Lucy's blonde hair and green eyes made her stand out in the crowd of brown-eyed island children. They were all silent in attention as she held up her sketches, describing the details of each insect. She'd taken particular care in illustrating all the insects' body parts: legs, wings, eyes, antennae, head, thorax, and abdomen. Since the children on the island had never seen a science book, they were curious to see the foreign insects in Lucy's drawings. Seeing their enthusiasm, she promised to bring some live specimens the next time.

When it came to the question and answer time, all the students raised their hands. Lucy panicked since she didn't know any of their names. It was Mrs. McBeal that eventually called on each pupil so Lucy could answer their questions, with a little exaggeration of her adventures.

When she finished, she stood waiting next to the window for Elizabeth. Across the village clearing she noticed the islanders gathering around Kalani. His voice rose loud above the chatter. Lucy headed down the school steps. She heard Kalani's voice shouting so she stopped to pause. Mrs. McBeal followed her to thank her for her presentation. "Such fine documentation, Lucy," she praised. "Yeh have demonstrated a superb talent fer scientific research."

"Thank you very much for inviting me here today," Lucy replied, staring out across the clearing in the village. The elders were sitting in front of a grass hut and Kalani's body swaying back and forth with his arms pointing to the forest as he roared to the men.

Just then Elizabeth arrived and the three of them stood watching the commotion.

"What's going on?" asked Lucy.

"Somethin' ter do with the *taro* fields and water," explained Elizabeth.

"Kalani's very angry," observed Lucy.

"Aye, I've never seen him act this way. Somethin' must be terribly wrong."

Suddenly, one of the elders stood up. He reached over and pushed Kalani backwards. Lucy watched as another man stood, grabbed Kalani's wrist, and led him to the *kahuna*'s hut. He pushed Kalani through a doorway draped with *tapa* cloth, and he was out of sight.

"Well, that's that," shrugged Elizabeth. "Probably somethin' ter do with the fish catch yesterday."

"How could that be? They caught thousands of fish," asked Lucy. "With that many, we will be eating fish forever. I'm getting nauseous just thinking about it."

"Yeh don' have ter worry about that, Lucy," laughed Mrs. McBeal. "I prefer chicken and pork. I only accept the fish because it's polite, that's all."

"Fantastic," smiled Lucy, "Isn't this the day Leah bakes the bread for the week?"

"Aye," replied Elizabeth.

"Then I'll race you to the house!" challenged Lucy.

"And the loser has ter help Leah with the dishes," said Elizabeth.

Both girls ran across the clearing to the forest path when Lucy called out, "Better get your apron, because I intend to win." Lucy was leading easily by a head, leaving Elizabeth breathless.

Twenty-Three

THE CONSPIRACY

The changes in seasons were different on the islands than in England. With autumn approaching, storms often churned in the clouds above and dumped rain for days. No one could predict when this would happen.

Lucy had grown accustomed to the fluctuations in the daily weather patterns.

Every morning, she looked forward to the crisp air that brought with it the subtle fragrance of flowering blossoms and the aroma of Leah's cooking. By lunchtime however, the air began to stir into a gentle breeze. In the late afternoon, it grew into a strong northerly wind that toppled flowerpots and slammed the windows and doors. Today, the morning was quiet except for a bird chorus coming from the tree outside the kitchen windows.

It was Lucy's job to arrange the breakfast settings on the long kitchen table. She placed a plate, a saucer, and a tea cup for each of the seven member household.

She had just finished placing the forks on the table when Reverend McBeal and her father entered the room.

"Good morning, Papa," greeted Lucy.

Lately, her father seemed to be angry. For all the years that Lucy lived in Ebley, she never once saw him unraveled. But since he took on the planning of the new settlement, every day was full of frustration and tension. He was becoming a different person, and she missed his gentleness.

"Good morning, Lucy," her father replied courteously, but his mind was on the conversation with Oliver's father. "Reverend McBeal! You mean to tell me there's another retaining wall?" snapped the Bishop. "How can they continue to defy us, and rebuild every night? Have them removed the boulders again this morning, I say. That will teach them to interfere with God's work."

"I have made plans for Kalani to escort Elizabeth and the children into the *hala* forest on the bluff over Mokea cave," the Revered interjected.

"Do you think that is the solution to our problems?" asked Bishop Tuppins.

"With Kalani out of the village, Burles will get the islanders' cooperation. I'm sure of it," the Reverend nodded.

Lucy looked up. A sound like a herd of running elephants thumped along the upstairs hallway, down the stairs, and into the kitchen. It turned out to be only Oliver and Eugene racing each other to the breakfast table. They bounded into the room followed by Elizabeth and Mrs. McBeal.

"Why, Lucy," said Mrs. McBeal, "looks like yeh've set a fine table this mornin'."

Lucy was pleased to receive such a wonderful compliment. However, her attention shifted to Elizabeth at that very moment. The young woman was slowly circling the table without uttering a single word. Lucy wondered what she was up to. At each place setting, Elizabeth lifted the cups and saucers.

"There aren' any insects hidin' under our cups, are there?" She raised an eyebrow, smiled, and looked directly at Lucy.

Lucy swallow hard. Then with a wink, she replied, "Only the digestible kind."

Everyone laughed, even her father. Then they all sat down around the table.

Out of nowhere, a green frog jumped onto Elizabeth's plate. Everyone looked at the croaker in surprise. Then all eyes turned to Oliver.

"Not my fault," he pleaded, trying to catch the creature. The frog jumped in and out of cups trying to escape Oliver's reach.

"Oliver, look what you've done, now. I'll have to wash everything before we eat!" Lucy was horrified. She lifted her apron, bent over the table, and scooped the frog up with one quick movement.

"Lucy, take that creature out of doors; and be sure to wash your hands," instructed the Bishop.

"Yes, Papa," she replied. Lucy knew that if she hadn't acted quickly, the poor frog would have been squished flat by Mrs. McBeal's broom.

Once everything had settled down and the eating had begun, Reverend McBeal cleared his throat. "Elizabeth, my dear," he started, "we don' have enough mats fer the church floor." He took a rather large bite of muffin, and chewed before continuing. "So I've made arrangements for Kalani ter escort yeh and the other children ter the *hala* forest ter collect more branches."

"But father," objected Elizabeth, "I have prepared a very important lesson fer the day. Can't we stay here?"

"This is very important too, young lady," Reverend McBeal replied.

"Besides, I'm sure Eugene and Oliver would enjoy a day off," added Mrs. McBeal, helping her husband's scheme along. "The lesson can wait 'til tomorrow mornin'."

Elizabeth knew that when her parents teamed up, there was no point in trying to change their minds. "So, Lucy, are yeh ready fer a new adventure?" she said resigned.

"I'm looking forward to it," the young girl answered, grinning broadly.

Twenty-Four

A Hurricane

Kalani arrived later that morning carrying a large sack over his shoulder full of tools. Not only did he have to harvest the *hala*, Kalani and the children had to haul them back to the village so that the women could weave mats for the church. It was a big job and would take most of the day.

"Hello, Kalani," greeted Elizabeth. She, Oliver, Eugene, and Lucy were waiting for him on the *lanai*. The notion of spending an entire afternoon with Kalani made her very happy. Even if she had to make a trip into the *hala* forest and put up with her little tag-a-long brothers, it was worth it if she got to be with the boy she loved.

Kalani led the group on a journey that took them miles from the settlement. Elizabeth wasn't used to walking long distances, but she forged along watching Kalani's brown skin shine in the afternoon sun. He looked so handsome with his dark hair tossing side to side as he marched down the forest path.

After several hours, they arrived at the high bluff over the Mokea cave.

Lucy looked down the mountain and could see the islanders building the bridges. "They look like tiny brown ants busy at work in their colony."

Up the slope of the great volcano, Kalani led them. They could see out across the vast ocean where millions of whitecaps dotted the blue water.

Elizabeth explained to Lucy that there were other islands that stretched north and south for fifty miles. Some were large and some quite small. They were part of a long volcanic chain that pushed up from the earth's floor, spewing red-hot lava from the depths below. It took thousands of years for each mound of rock to eventually become a lush, green paradise island.

Finally, the group reached the *hala* grove. Elizabeth eased herself down onto an old tree stump to rest while Kalani prepared to cut the branches.

"Elizabeth," Lucy said, laying out the blanket for a picnic lunch, "is Kalani in trouble?"

The elder girl perked up at the question. "Why? What do yeh mean, trouble?"

Lucy hesitated a moment before saying, "This morning in the kitchen, I overheard something." She began unloading the picnic basket they brought, unsure if she should say anymore.

"Well, out with it," prompted Elizabeth.

"They were planning to send Kalani away," Lucy said as she set out the muffins, jam, and chicken.

"I don' understand," Elizabeth replied, her face crunching up in confusion.

"Yesterday, the elders wouldn't listen to me," said Kalani, sliding down from a nearby palm tree. He came over to the girls and stuffed a muffin into his mouth from the food Lucy laid out. "*Hoku* says to me that I'm the son of the Chief. That means I'm a threat."

"Then there is trouble," gasped Elizabeth.

"Twice, the *taro* fields have been destroyed because of Burles. But twice the *Menehune* rebuilt them to save the *taro*. My people are frightened about what is going to happen next," explained Kalani, peeling the sides of a fruit with his front teeth.

"But surely, yeh cannot stop him all by yehrself?" Elizabeth mused.

Kalani continued, "This *haole* man, Burles, will take our land and water from us; and he doesn't care how he does it."

"Are yeh sure?" concern crept into Elizabeth's voice.

"Elizabeth, you are well educated, but naïve. My eyes don't deceive me." Kalani smiled wryly at his love.

"He's right, Elizabeth," warned Lucy, placing her hand over the pouch dangling from her waist. "Burles is as evil as they come."

Kalani gazed absently at the ground. "We are one with the *'aina*. This is what our ancestors have taught us. If the land hurts, a part of our soul is hurt. You cannot separate the two."

"Well then, yeh must report this ter yehr father," advised Elizabeth.

A heavy sign escaped Kalani. "My father is blinded by beautiful silks and intoxicating drink."

Eugene and Oliver finally arrived at the picnic spot. They had been exploring the tunnels behind the grove, and decided to come and see if lunch was ready.

"Oh, it's nice ter see yeh two. Oliver, did Eugene get yeh lost?" laughed Elizabeth.

"I have my compass, so never fear. See? That's north and that's south," declared Oliver, pointing out over the ocean.

"Very funny," scoffed Eugene. "I'm not the one who's challenged directionally."

"We saw you in the village yesterday," Lucy continued with Kalani. "Won't the elders help you sort this out?"

"Their ears are closed," replied Kalani. "But there will be a day others will follow me. *Hoku* says that I must wait with patience." He turned back to his task and climbed another tall wobbly gray tree trunk with no effort at all. "This has many *hala*. Right over here is a good tree for climbing."

"What can I do?" asked Oliver, jumping up and down on the ground below.

"Stay out from under the tree fer starters," said Elizabeth, pulling him to the side. "Use that brain the good Lord gave yeh."

"Can I join you up there?" called Lucy, looking at Kalani.

"No. Take Oliver with you into the gulch. There are plenty of Noni berries to gather – good medicine," he replied.

The gulch had steep walls formed out of layers of rock. When water from the heavy storms spilled out over the high bluff on the mountainside, it only had one place to go – the gulch below. The runoff water would crash down like a river, pushing boulders the size of houses into the valleys below. During the recent draught however, the gulch had grown full of brush and low-lying trees.

The children had been taking their time, climbing down the sides of the rocks, and finally reached the gulch floor below.

"I don' know if I like the idea of them goin' down there alone," called Elizabeth, trying to get Kalani's attention.

"Listen, that girl can take care of Oliver and herself. I'm sure of it," said Eugene, jumping out of the way of a falling branch.

"Lucy doesn't need to fear," Kalani called down. "She is surrounded by a good spirit, *uhane.*"

"Great!" exclaimed Eugene, rolling his eyes. "Now she's some sort of Joan of Arc."

"Enough, Eugene!" snapped Elizabeth. She bent down to assist her brother in dragging a huge branch over to the cave's entrance.

Kalani continued slicing at the tree with his large knife. After a while, Elizabeth and Eugene had dragged over enough *hala* to fill a freight car.

They were all working so hard that they hadn't noticed the sky. It was a dirty gray, growing darker and darker by the minute.

Eugene looked down at his watch and wondered if it was time to begin the journey back. "Hey! What's goin' on up there," he asked, pointing to the sky. "It's only three o'clock. Why is the sky turning black?"

Kalani stopped hacking and slid around the tree trunk to look out at the ocean. The other islands had disappeared through the dense, low-moving clouds and a hotter than normal breeze wafted past him with smells of dead fish.

"*Kona* wind," said Kalani. "Comes from the south. There's a storm headed this way."

"That doesn' sound very encouragin'," remarked Elizabeth.

A gust of wind blew so hard just then that it whipped the trunk of the tree back and forth and Kalani had to hold on with all his might. Elizabeth felt raindrops fall on her forehead. Quickly she ran to steady the base of the tree while Kalani cautiously descended.

"This isn' good," she said. "I think we'd better head fer home, now!"

"There's no time," Kalani replied urgently, reaching the ground. "We need to find shelter."

The wind grew stronger, and Elizabeth grabbed onto the back of Eugene's vest. As the clouds swirled above, the wind blew the *hala* branches away. Fighting against the gusts, Elizabeth pulled Eugene toward the tunnel opening. As the trio reached the safety of the cave, Kalani, Eugene, and Elizabeth huddled closely together out of the wind.

Twenty-Five

An Albatross

"Lucy! She's still in the gulch with Oliver," Elizabeth realized after a moment. She looked frantically at her companions.

"Stay here, Eugene," ordered Kalani. He took Elizabeth's hand. "You, follow me."

Raindrops blew sideways and felt like tiny razors slicing Elizabeth's delicate pink cheeks. She was terrified but trusted that Kalani knew what he was doing and where they were going. Reaching the edge of the cliff, Elizabeth held onto Kalani as he braced them both against a firmly-rooted bush.

"Lucy!" shouted Kalani, searching the crevasse below. "Can you hear me?"

"Yes, I can hear you!" Lucy replied, her tiny body appearing among the brush. "It is fantastic down here! Just like an enchanted forest."

"Well, yehr enchanted forest is about ter turn into a gruesome deluge any minute now!" shouted Elizabeth over the roar of the wind.

"Where's Oliver?" called Kalani.

"I'm over here!" hollered Oliver, also appearing out of the brush.

Elizabeth watched as the trickling stream of water beneath Kalani's feet quickly expanded. The rains from the mountain top had reached the bluff and the raging water was on its way toward them.

"Oliver, climb up fast!" commanded Kalani, pushing Elizabeth further into the security of the bush. Then, using a vine as a rope, he lowered himself down as far as he could onto a small ledge and reached down for Oliver.

The young boy scampered up the rocky wall and grabbed Kalani's hand. The young man lifted Oliver the rest of the way and secured him to the end of the vine. With one strong pull, Kalani hoisted the boy up towards his sister. The rain was pouring now, and torrents spilled over every ledge. Elizabeth reached for Oliver while Kalani continued to cling to the rocks below.

Just as she secured her brother, Elizabeth's muddy feet slipped and the rushing water dragged her over the outcropping above Kalani. She screamed and tried to hold onto anything she could find, digging her fingers deep into the mud. A gush of water threatened to make her fall when she felt Kalani's strong hand. He grabbed her shoulder, and pulled her up with him. He held her tight.

"Yeh're my guardian angel," she said, looking into his brown eyes.

Huddled together with Oliver, their eyes searched the gulch below. It had become a rising river. Then they spotted Lucy's yellow curls.

"Lucy, hang on!" Elizabeth called. "Yeh'll be alright!"

Kalani snatched a low-hanging vine, and prepared to swing cross the ravine down to Lucy when they heard her small voice cry out, "I'm so cold!"

A violent wind tossed the little girl's body into the bushes, where her legs got peppered with scratches. She heard Kalani calling her name and tried getting her legs to work. Lucy took a deep breath and forced herself to get up, bracing her legs against the flow around her.

Lucy panicked as the water rose above her knees. She knew that she needed to climb higher. Up ahead Lucy noticed that a tree had fallen. Maybe, just maybe, she could get to it and climb up above all the flooding. Her heart beating faster and faster as her fear rose along with the water level.

Just as she reached the tree, a surge of water plummeted down the cliff-face and flooded the gulch even more. Lucy saw the bushes disappear quickly under the water. She wrapped her arms around a large branch, and held on tight.

The aching cold water crept up into her shoes, then over her knees, and finally covered her shoulders.

Lucy clinging to a branch of the fallen tree trunk, she kept her eyes shut, trying to close out the terror. Images of the Ebley River drifted into her mind, and she let out a helpless whimper. She felt a tug on her neck, and when she opened her eyes, she saw that her locket and chain had come out from under her dress. The locket floated on the surface of the water beneath her nose.

For a moment, Lucy's heart stopped pounding. She gasped for air, her chest pushing against the force of the water.

Then Kalani's voice came through the wind. "Hold tight!" he yelled. "I'm almost there!"

She looked above her head and saw him swinging down towards her. She stretched up a hand to reach out for him.

Crack!

The bough she clung to broke away from the tree and dragged her away from Kalani and further into the depths of the raging gulch.

There was nothing more Kalani could do to get to Lucy. He watched in dismay as her tiny body, clinging to the limb, floated off into the distance. The rain continued to pour down upon their heads, and Elizabeth fought back tears of sadness as Lucy disappeared toward the valley.

Kalani said a silent prayer to God that Lucy would be alright, realizing that he did all that he could do. He made his way back to Oliver and Elizabeth on the ledge and the three of them climbed back up to the top of the gulch. He knew it wasn't safe to remain out in the open, so he led them through the heavy wind and rain to the shelter of the tunnel.

Meanwhile, Lucy bobbed up and down in the dark, cold rapids, her arms growing numb by the frigid flowing current.

She fought back her tears. They were no good to her now. Being clear headed was her only chance for survival.

"Dear Lord in heaven," she prayed, "keep me safe."

Up ahead, there were clumps of vines and branches growing out of the stone. As the tree limb swirled towards them, she reached out to grab a vine.

But the current pulled her away.

Her hopes crushed, Lucy went back to laying on her belly, straddling the tree limb. She couldn't feel it anymore because her legs and toes had gone completely numb from the cold. The tears threatened to come again when she caught sight of something. Trailing on the water's surface nearby was her locket, still dangling from the chain around her neck.

Lucy forced herself to release her stiff grip and reach for the trinket, but the current shifted and she had to cling to the limb before it smashed into a rock wall. It took all of her strength to keep herself on the tiny makeshift lifeboat. Frightened that she would lose the locket, she watched it swirling next to her just out of reach. She felt the chain around her neck go taut, and then *SNAP!* Her locket, chain, and the memory of her mother disappeared in the churning water.

"No, no, no," she pleaded in a soft hoarse voice. But there was no one to hear her cries.

Rain continued to pour out of the sky, ravaging everything. Lucy's arms shivered and grew weak. Although she held on firmly, her grip was slipping. The limb kept dipping under the flood and coming back up, and each time Lucy caught her breath, she tried to call out. But eventually when she opened her mouth, there was no sound. Her locket was lost, and she was sure she would drown. So, she closed her eyes and prepared herself to let go.

Out of the black skies, a gigantic bird flew through the torrential rain. It glided over the ledge and deep into the gully, looking for something. It tilted its head from side to side, peering down. Then, tucking its long wings, it dropped through the air like a hawk after prey.

Just as she released her grip on the limb, Lucy felt something snatch the back of her dress and raise her from the water. She blinked her eyes open, and saw the deep ravine whizzing past, filled with churning water and debris. The cliff sides were saturated, and great stone ledges began to crumble above them. The bird tried to fly higher, dodging back and forth, but there were too many boulders. Lucy heard a loud thump and then she was falling with the bird. They both hit the ravine wall and tumbled down until they landed on a flat surface just above the waterline.

With her lungs still full of water, Lucy coughed and gagged as she lay on the ledge. She turned her head, and found herself staring directly into the bird's eye. He blinked and Lucy smiled. She was amazed that not only was she alive, but the bird was too. "Hold on, you're alright!"

Lucy looked around at her surroundings. She was really happy that she was there and that she didn't drown. Above her head was a small overhang in front of a large opening in the rock. She rolled over, and sat up.

The enormous bird made it to his feet, and waddled back and forth. Lucy giggled when he shook his wings, sending water droplets flying through the air. He turned and nodded his head toward the opening to a cave.

"In there? Doesn't look very inviting," she said uncertainly, peering into the entrance. Lucy stood up and walked over for a closer inspection. "But it is dry!"

She turned just in time to see the bird fly back out into the storm.

"Wait!" she called after it. "I didn't' have a chance to thank you for saving my life!"

The fantastic gray bird soared out of the gulch and into the darkness of the clouds.

Lucy walked further into the cave and followed the long tunnel ahead. She made her way hand-over-hand, feeling the cold stone walls through the pitch darkness. Although she was trembling and exhausted, she was very glad to still be alive.

After a while, she came to a clearing and decided to sit on the ground and rest for a while. Pulling her knees up to her chest, she wondered if the bird saving her had been a dream. Her eye lids grew heavy, and before she knew it, Lucy Tuppins was fast asleep in the darkness.

Twenty-Six

Mokea Cave

Lucy woke the next morning feeling a little sore. She was in a large cavern under the forest floor. Roots and sunshine peeked through tiny holes in the ceiling, and she could hear the sound of a river flowing just beyond the boulders. At her feet was a warm bed of cinders leftover from a small campfire. She was wrapped from head to toe in a rough piece of fabric.

She was confused. Was Kalani there? Was it he who wrapped her up? And where had he gone off to? Lucy leaned forward, rubbing her hands together over the warm coals. As she looked around, she became aware that the cavern was deserted. But she noticed a line of stones trailing away from the fire pit and around the boulders.

Lucy followed them and found that they led up a gradual incline to a hole in the ceiling. There was also a red reflection dancing around the cave in the morning's light.

She traced it to a red stone at the base the small path leading up to the hole. After picking it up and rubbing it on her dress, she discovered that the source of the red flashes was a gold ring with a gem the size of a cherry.

Maybe it was the ring of a pirate, she thought excitedly. *But Kalani never told me of any pirates.* She wondered if it might be possible because she'd read about Spanish and French pirates who commandeered vessels in the Caribbean waters. The ring would have to be researched. Lucy smiled to herself; she always liked a new challenge.

She stuffed the ring down into her purse, climbed up the small incline, and crawled out of the hole in the ceiling.

Lucy stood high on a bluff, overlooking the gulch below. It was full of trees and huge rocks. She was very glad not to have drowned down there.

Then she heard the sounds of familiar voices coming from the path below.

"I'm never goin' ter forgive myself fer lettin' her climb down into that gulch," sobbed Elizabeth, blowing her nose into a mud-stained hankie.

"She was a great sport," said Eugene, patting Elizabeth on the back to comfort her. "I was getting' ter like her a little, too."

"Swept out ter sea she is," sniffed Oliver.

Lucy stood just a few yards above, eaves dropping on the conversation. "Hello, are you looking for someone?" she giggled and smiled down at them.

Elizabeth gasped. She thought she had heard a ghost. They all looked up. "Oh, praise the good saints, she's alive!

It's our Lucy!" exclaimed Elizabeth. When they saw the little blonde girl, they took off running to greet her with hugs and kisses.

"Yeh're dry," marveled Kalani, pulling at her stained yellow dress, "so you were safe after all!"

"Yes, thank you for covering me up with the blanket," Lucy replied. "And the trail of stones was a good idea. I found my way out of the cave just fine."

"It wasn't me," Kalani shook his head. "I bet it was the *Menehune*. They are guardians of the lost."

"What?" the little girl perked up. "No! I missed them?"

Kalani explained, "We don't see them, but still we know they are there."

"See, I told yeh they weren't imaginary," mocked Oliver, poking Eugene in the ribs.

"You have *uhane*, Lucy," said Kalani, bending down placing his hands on her shoulders. "You're very special, and the *Menehune* will protect you."

"Well, wait 'til you hear the rest of it. There was this-," she began, but Elizabeth interrupted Lucy with a tone of urgency in her voice.

"I'd love ter hear yehr story Lucy, but right now is not a good time," she explained, lifting her skirt partway to reveal a leaf tied around her leg.

"She's been hurt," Eugene said. "We have ter get her back home."

Lucy looked down at the swollen leg concerned. "Will she be alright?"

Kalani helped Elizabeth start down the hill. "I did what I could do for her now, but there is an urgency so we need to head for home now."

Lucy, Oliver, and Eugene trailed behind the couple. She glanced at Eugene and teased, "Eugene, did I hear you say that you are actually starting to like me?"

He wasn't amused and quickly clarified his intentions by saying, "I said it because everyone was feelin' bad about yehr drownin'. It doesn't mean a thin'. Don' go gettin' any ideas in that head of yehrs that we are best friends or anythin' like that!"

Their parents were very happy to see the children when they arrived back home that afternoon, although Mrs. McBeal ordered them to remain outside for a late breakfast. The children sat at the table in the backyard, their hair and clothes still caked in mud. They recounted their adventures in yesterday's storm while they filled their stomachs with Leah's good cooking.

Oliver handed Lucy a guava and asked, "Tell me," he mumbled, chewing on a mango muffin, "what did the *Menehune* look like?"

Lucy shook her head. "I told you, I never saw them. What I did see was this fantastic bird."

"Good Lord, we don' want ter hear about no more bugs, birds, or whatever else yeh research," Eugene was getting annoyed at how much she went on about creatures. He picked up his plate and moved to the end of the table, as far away as he possibly could be without leaving the table altogether.

Lucy didn't care if Eugene wanted to be in his own world. "Oliver?" she asked. "Have you ever seen a huge gray bird with the wings of an angel?"

"Aye, once," he replied. "Called an albatross. But they live on another island. Don' see them around these parts."

"Well, what if I told you I saw one?"

"Where?" Oliver asked.

"Picked me right up out of the water yesterday." Lucy pulled on the back of her dress where the bird had nabbed her.

"And they say I'm a teller of tales!" laughed Oliver.

"Then don't believe me," Lucy frowned, folding her arms on her chest. "I don't care." She wanted to share with them all her discoveries, but was getting frustrated at their lack of enthusiasm about her research.

She reached into her purse and pulled out the ring. It made a clinking sound when she set it on the table.

"Blimey," breathed Oliver, his eyes bulging out of his head.

"Good Lord, Lucy!" exclaimed Eugene, glancing over at them and seeing the red gem. "Yeh'd find a pot of gold at the end of some rainbow, if yeh had a mind to!" He walked over, and picked up the ring.

"So, now you are interested?" she asked, turning toward Eugene. "I found it in the cave yesterday."

"I bet a pirate lost it," said Oliver, his eyes still fixed on the ring.

"Aha! That's exactly what I thought," Lucy agreed wholeheartedly.

"Now what would a pirate be doin' on this island?" asked Eugene.

Oliver snatched the ring from Eugene to examine it more closely for himself. After a moment his eyebrows scrunched up and he murmured, "Think I've seen this before."

"Where?" Lucy asked.

"On Burles."

"Well, that blows yehr pirate theory right ter the depths of the sea," said Eugene, wrinkling his nose at Lucy and sitting down across from her this time.

Yes, now that she thought about it, she did remember seeing it on Burles finger when he grabbed her on the ship.

"What would he be doin' in that cave?" Eugene wondered out loud. The three children thought hard for a minute.

"What if the coin on the ship and the coin I found in the forest were part of a treasure?" Lucy posited. "You yourself said that it was not any currency you'd ever seen," she continued, looking at Eugene.

He grabbed the ring back from Oliver and placed it on his thumb. It was too big and slipped off, falling onto the table.

"Look, what's this?" he asked, pointing to an inscription engraved on the inside of the gold band.

"Let me see," demanded Lucy, leaning down for a better look. "Isn't that a royal family crest?"

"We could ask father; he'd know," suggested Oliver.

Lucy and Eugene bolted up at the same time and bumped their foreheads together as they both yelled out, "No!"

"Oliver, you have to promise to keep all of this a secret until we've got more facts," Lucy pleaded.

"Oh, all right," sighed Oliver, slouching on the bench.

The ring was placed back in the purse. As the children finished eating, they came to a decision. After lunch and some warm baths, they would search the books in the study for clues about the ring.

Twenty-Seven

The Secret of the Ring

That afternoon the house was empty, all but for Mrs. McBeal, Eugene, Oliver, and Lucy. There were no visitors coming and going like usual, and the children could hear her plunking away at the small piano in the dining room.

"Why do yeh suppose Burles is workin' fer yehr father?" asked Eugene standing on a small step stool in the study. "If he has the coins, he'd be rich." He sneezed as he pulled a dusty brown book off the top shelf.

"Probably stole this ring right off the Queen's fat finger," commented Oliver, holding it up and squinting at the gem in the light.

"No, I'm afraid not," explained Lucy. "The treasure was stolen out of the palace cellar vault. And besides, the Queen was asleep in her own room."

The volume was placed on the desk, and Eugene began to thumb through the pages. Finally, Eugene came upon the illustrations he was looking for. "Burles had been pushin' the islanders really hard ter get the settlement finished. Don' suppose he's plannin' ter leave with the Tahiti ship, do yeh?"

"That's it!" exclaimed Lucy. "Hired by father in England, it looks as if he was here on a real job. It's the perfect alibi."

"No one would suspect a connection ter a remote island like Maui, "added Eugene.

"Except us," cut in Oliver. "Lucy has the coin."

"Aye, but yeh promised, Oliver," reminded Eugene, "Don' say anythin'."

"Mum's the word, a secret is as good as gold with me!" assured Oliver.

"Here it is," pointed out Eugene excitedly, placing the ring next to its entry.

The three children leaned over the book. Lucy deciphered the tiny print under a picture of the ring.

"Says here that the crest belongs to the House of Burleigh?" she said. "How did Burles get the ring?"

"Must have been in the vault," shrugged Eugene.

"I don't think so," said Lucy, shaking her head. "You see, Burles was wearing it. If he stole it, why would he wear it out in the open for everyone to see?"

"I think it's because he's all muscle and no brains," replied Eugene.

Oliver picked up the ring and shoved it over his tiny plump thumb. "I'd wear it, if I found it."

"He didn't find it, he stole it," insisted Lucy. "Now give it back."

Oliver reluctantly returned the ring, placing it on the desk.

"I wouldn' be too sure about that; look here," said Eugene, reading to the next page. "It's the lineage chart of the House of Burleigh. And here it says, 'The House of Burleigh, originated in Wales in the early 1300's with Edward Burleigh. Settled in Stanton-Upon-Edge. Lord George Edward Burleigh, appointed England's treasurer under the Queen in 1810'!"

"Edward Burles Burleigh," Lucy continued to read. "'Born 1795 in London, first born son of Lord Burleigh'."

"He's Lord Burleigh's son!" gasped Eugene, closing the book. "He's already rich. Why would he have ter rob the Queen?"

"And to think he is going to let his father hang for the crime!" cried Lucy.

They all stood quietly for a moment, trying to absorb the magnitude of it all. The sound of someone clearing her throat startled the trio and made them spin around. The children had been so wrapped up in their investigation, that they hadn't heard Mrs. McBeal walk into the study.

She eyed them suspiciously, with her hands on her hips. "And just what are yeh children up ter?" she inquired.

Lucy reached very slowly behind her for the ring on the desk and clenched it tightly in the palm of her hand.

Eugene stalled for time so that Lucy could secure the ring. He moved forward to block his mother's view of the desk. "Lucy was just helpin' me research an assignment," lied Eugene.

Glad they were finally getting along, Mrs. McBeal said, "She's the best," and winked in Lucy's direction. "Yeh'll learn a thin' or two from this lassie."

"Oh, I think I have, mam," Eugene agreed to readily. He glanced back to see if the ring was hidden yet. Lucy slid her hand down into her purse, depositing the jewel without Mrs. McBeal's notice.

The children stood still like statues, watching Mrs. McBeal browse through the bookshelves and remove a book.

"Now off ter the washroom with yeh," she ordered, waving at the children. "Supper's nearly ready."

The three scampered off just as the other members of the household returned.

When the meal was over, Bishop Tuppins and Reverend McBeal retired outside onto the *lanai* with Mrs. McBeal.

"Have yeh given much thought ter takin' a wife again, Bishop?" asked the Reverend.

Bishop Tuppins shook his head. "Been too busy with the new settlement to worry about such matters."

"That child of yehrs could use a strong woman's hand," said Mrs. McBeal.

"When the time comes, I'm sure there are several good Christian women the church can recommend back home," the Bishop replied, trying to end this line of conversation.

"I hope that yeh don' think us presumptuous, but the Mrs. here and I have put a lot of thought into what we are about ter say," continued the Reverend.

"Why go lookin' for someone who yeh have no knowledge of? Yeh need someone yeh already know, someone who works with children, and has good character ter bring ter the marriage," argued Mrs. McBeal.

"What my dear wife is tryin' ter say," explained the Reverend, "is that yeh don' have ter go lookin' across the ocean when there is a suitable candidate right here amongst us."

The Bishop choked on his lemonade. "I don't intend on taking an islander as a wife!" he sputtered.

"No, no," said Reverend McBeal. "We just want yeh ter know that our daughter Elizabeth would be a fine candidate if and when yeh decide ter take another wife."

Bishop Tuppins sat frozen and speechless at the suggestion. He'd never considered a second wife so soon. Just then, Lucy and Elizabeth ran out of the house, playing a game of tag. Elizabeth grabbed Lucy around the waist and lifted her into the air.

"I won!" the young woman laughed. Lucy giggled when Elizabeth put her down and tickled her.

"What is it, Papa?" asked Lucy, when she saw the troubled look on her father's face.

"Nothing," he replied, dismissing his thoughts. Bishop Tuppins stared at them still trying to grasp the idea of a new wife. "Come now and give me a hug before bed. You must be exhausted from the day."

"Good night mam, father," Elizabeth said. Then she nodded toward the Bishop. "Good night, sir."

As soon as the girls returned into the house, the Bishop started up the conversation again. But this time the subject was an entirely different and a more pressing matter than finding a wife.

"We'll never make the deadline with all the damage from the storm," he said.

"Do yeh think this land might be possessed by some evil demons who steal into the night?" asked the Reverend.

"Absolutely not!" assured the Bishop. "The storm wiped out the bridge and set us back a day, that's all."

"How do yeh explain the new bridge, then? Just appeared overnight, it did!" replied the Reverend.

"I agree with you, it is suspicious," said the Bishop. "We want the water for the farms and the islanders want the water for their *taro*. It isn't a stretch of the imagination to think that they could be the ones sabotaging the entire project. Maybe it was the islanders, not an evil demon."

"Have yeh considered the legend?" asked the Reverend.

"What legend?"

"The legend of the *Menehune*," the Reverend clarified.

Mrs. McBeal shook her head as she took up her sewing. "All this talk about demons and legends. Leave that ter the islanders. Our faith is in God."

"Yeh're right, woman. Have I told yeh that I'm truly blessed to have yeh here with me?" asked the Reverend, kissing his wife on the cheek.

Twenty-Eight

Hawaiian Healer

It was the start of another day when Lucy opened the shutters to look out across the branches of the climbing tree. She was glad to be alive, but still couldn't shake the sadness of losing her locket.

"Mum," she whispered into the breeze, "I'm going to find you, I promise."

She fought back the tears that wanted to roll down her cheeks as she put on a clean dress. Then she took a few deep breaths as she buttoned up her shoes. Feeling calmer and more confident, Lucy tied the purse around her waist. There were three clues tucked safely inside, and she couldn't wait to discover more. However, her first priority was to get back to the gulch to find her locket.

It was Friday, two days after their perilous journey into the *hala* forest. The household was silent with the absence of adults and the boys. Lucy and Elizabeth had been left to get some extra sleep.

The little girl knocked on her friend's door and peeked into the room. She was surprised to find that Elizabeth was still in bed. The shutters were still shut, so Lucy crossed the room and pushed them open to let in the morning sun."

"A fine lady you've become!" she teased. "Sleeping until noon, are we?"

Elizabeth lifted the pillow from behind and quickly pulled it down over her head. She muttered from under the pillow, "I'm exhausted, Lucy; let me sleep. Leave me alone."

Lucy sat on the end of the bed lazily, pulling her calves up to her thighs and crossing her ankles.

"Are you alright?" asked Lucy. A strange odor wafted up the little girl's nose. She sniffed the air for a moment. There was a horrible smell coming from the bed, so she pinched her nose closed.

"And I suppose yeh're not a bit tired after our little adventure in the forest?" asked Elizabeth.

"Not me. Come on, get out from under those covers," Lucy insisted, peeling the sheet off Elizabeth's body.

"Lucy, look!" gasped Elizabeth, sitting up in alarm. She stared at her swollen red leg and the oozing gash just below her knee.

"You've got an infection. I've seen that sort of thing before," Lucy said.

Elizabeth began to cry. "We're all alone in the house; what are we goin' ter do?"

"Blubbering won't help," urged Lucy, pulling at Elizabeth's arms. "We've got to see the *kahuna*. He'll know what to do."

Elizabeth sucked in a breath. "Father will be furious. He says the man's a witch doctor."

"Well, I suppose I could just leave you here," frowned Lucy, abruptly releasing Elizabeth's arms. "And then your fever will spike, you will become delirious, eventually unconscious, and possibly die before supper." Lucy covering her mouth and pretended to be fainting from grief.

"Oh, for heaven's sake," sighed Elizabeth, rolling her eyes. She got out of bed and began changing into her dress.

The girls slowly made their way to the village since Elizabeth's leg was in pain. The moment Kalani saw his love, he ran over to greet her. She was pale and sweating, and when she looked up into his face, her body sagged in relief as she fainted in his arms.

"We've come to see the *kahuna*," Lucy explained hurriedly. "She's got an infection."

Kalani lifted Elizabeth's limp body into his arms and rushed to the healer's hut, with Lucy close behind.

Hoku greeted them at the door of his hut. Inside, the walls and ceilings were draped with dried leaves. A familiar smell reminded Lucy of her grandmother. The hut grew dark as *Hoku* pulled the *tapa* cloth down over the entrance.

Elizabeth's body was placed on the mat in the center of the hut. When she opened her eyes, she saw Kalani leaning over her. His tender touch seemed to relax her, but she could see concern in his eyes. It had only been two days since he tended her wound while they were in the forest, and the infection was spreading rapidly.

Hoku and Kalani began chanting and singing. Lucy decided it's be best if she remained sitting out of the way in the corner of the hut. She watched as Kalani took out a stone pestle and began smashing *taro* root on a long wooden slab. *Hoku* continued to chant, moving around the room and selecting various leaves that hung from the rafters.

Maile poked her head into the hut. "Aloha," she said.

Lucy had never seen a healing ritual. She wondered if it was some kind of hocus pocus, just as her father had warned. But she took the offered bowl of *poi* from Maile anyways.

"We all eat," explained Maile to Lucy. "The big one is for the gods. They are here with us now."

The creamy substance slid off her fingers as Lucy attempted to scoop it up into her mouth.

"This is awful!" she whispered when she tasted it. Lucy let the yucky purple paste slide down her throat. It made her cough and gag.

"*Poi* is made from the *taro*," informed Maile. "Very good for you."

"*Taro?*" asked Lucy. "And this is what you are trying to save?" She coughed again and tried to swallow the lingering taste away. "It tastes pretty bad. Are you sure it is all that important?"

Maile took the bowl from Lucy, and began telling her the story about the plant. "The tale of how the *taro* came to us has been passed down many generations. Our ancestors said it was when the sky came down and met the land."

"Together they had a child, but it was born without any life," added Kalani.

"So they buried the child in a stream. Nourished by the water, it was not long before the child took on another form, and grew to be a *taro* plant," narrated Maile. "Now, the second child born to the sky and the land was man. We have a responsibility to take care of our brother, the *taro*."

Elizabeth was in great pain. Her knuckles turned white as she squeezed the mat, wincing as *Hoku* and Kalani applied an herbal salve to the wound. Then the two men laced a blanket of shiny *ti* leaves around Elizabeth. Lucy sincerely hoped that she had done the right thing in bringing Elizabeth to the healer.

"Someday, Kalani too, will know of the healing ways," said Maile. "Grandfather teaches him."

"It is good you came quickly," commented *Hoku*, bending down to place his large brown hand on Lucy's head.

"She won't die, will she?" Lucy asked anxiously.

Elizabeth turned her head and raised her arms into the air. "I'm right here! Yeh're talkin' as if I were already dead!" she exclaimed.

"Sorry," Lucy chuckled with a nervous guilt.

Hoku and Kalani gently wrapped Elizabeth's oozing sore with a *ti* leaf and finally placed a tapa cloth bandage around her leg. "Elizabeth, you will be alright," assured Kalani, placing a kiss on her forehead.

"Many are in danger this day," he turned to address the others. "The foreigner, *haole*, came into the village and took many of the young islanders."

"Why did he do that?" asked Lucy.

Kalani continued, "He is angry. The bridges that the workers built yesterday disappeared during the night."

"*Menehune*," explained *Hoku*. "Took down new bridges, built back old bridge over the *taro*."

"I don' understand," said Elizabeth as Hoku helped her to her feet. "How long is this tearin' down and rebuildin' goin' ter go on fer?"

"A week or so," replied Kalani.

Everyone in the hut watched Elizabeth stand on her legs unassisted. Maile explained that there was still an infection, but the herbal compress would cure her quickly.

"*E Holaihi'i nau*," said *Hoku*, reaching his long arms around Elizabeth in an affectionate hug.

"He says that you can leave now," translated Kalani.

Lucy jumped up. She'd been sitting a long time, and her feet were beginning to have that prickly feeling. She took Elizabeth by the hand and turned toward *Hoku* to thank him for helping her friend, "*Mahalo nui loa*."

Twenty-Nine

The Deadline

Late that night, the Bishop paced back and forth in the study. "It's less than a month now. What are we to do?"

Lucy heard his angry voice resonate throughout the house. She'd gotten used to his temper and continued to sit calmly in her room and brush her hair. But when the second voice boomed through the walls, she had to do something.

She tiptoed quickly out into the hallway, and crouched down behind the railing. The stench of Burles' cigar filled the air. She hated that smell.

"You're not the only one with a deadline," snapped Burles.

"Islanders building at night, bridges being moved, streams reappearing overnight," the Bishop sighed impatiently. "Excuses, excuses. When are you going to finish the job I hired you to do?"

"Listen, I've leaned on the Chief just about as hard as I can without raising suspicion," Burles said gruffly.

The door to the study opened.

Lucy froze.

She watched Burles' enormous shadow spilling across the floor. Dark arms moved back and forth from the shadow form, and Burles' finger pointing to the Bishop.

"Now it's up to you. Tell him to put a stop to all this. His people have to agree to the original settlement plans and start cooperating with us," the voice of the shadow grew louder.

"Me?" asked the Bishop incredulously. "What can I do at this point?"

The more Burles spoke, the more Lucy despised him. She knew he was lying. Tearing out the fields for the settlement expansion wouldn't benefit the islanders like Burles was proposing. Actually, the intent was to make way for a new community of Englishmen due to arrive on the next ship.

"The Chief has no spine. All he does is strut around pounding that stick of his. Someone has to convince him that he is a leader, and it's about time he started controlling his people – by force, if need be," stressed Burles. "And that someone is you."

A lump swelled up in Lucy's throat. She was afraid for her father. He used to be someone the people of the parish looked up to for comfort and compassion. Now he was a cruel person driven by ambition.

The next morning, every tree, bush, and plant left in the planned settlement area was uprooted. This path of destruction could be seen for miles. The land was now barren, stripped of the life that gave strength and nourishment to the islanders.

The Chief and Bishop Tuppins stood high above the settlement site. While it was true that the land was cleared, they still had to re-divert the stream and take down a bridge yet again before they could proceed.

The Bishop had no idea who was responsible for rebuilding the bridge over the taro fields. Four times, his crews had demolished it, and four times during the nights, it was rebuilt.

The Chief looked down at his people from the bluff as the workforce of fifty men, pulling at the ropes, brought the bridge structure crashing down. He was pleased with their strength and said, "Good workers."

The Bishop cleared his throat before replying. "I've been meaning to talk to you about that."

"Strong bridges," remarked the Chief.

"Well, yes. They are strong. But as you can see, we still only have one of the four proposed bridges built. We are wasting valuable time fooling around with this section." The Bishop waved his hand over the scene.

The Chief pointed. "Good water from the mountain."

Bishop Tuppins lost his patience. "See here. Aren't you *Ali'i*? Wise and powerful?"

The Chief turned away from the Bishop and asked, "Where's Burles? I want to talk with him."

Taking a breath to compose himself, the Bishop stepped around the Chief and replied, "He's not here today. Actually, he asked that I might speak with you."

"Burles said that he had more rum," growled the Chief.

"Yes, yes; he probably does. But, you must realize that new construction is impossible if your people keep putting back everything we tear down. So, I am very sorry, but you won't be seeing any more rum until they stop doing that. Two weeks, that's all the time we have." The Bishop got nervous as the seconds ticked by with no response from the Chief.

"No rum?" asked the leader as he turned and fixed the Bishop with an angry stare.

"Not until the last building is complete. Do you understand?" said the Bishop firmly.

The Chief didn't look happy but he nodded yes.

"Good, I'm glad we have all that straightened out," declared the Bishop.

Thirty

The Ruler of the Land

Several decades earlier, a powerful warrior roamed from island to island. Many of the village elders fought beside this great man who unified the islands. He became their king.

The village elders' stories of their legendary battles and bravery alongside King Kamehameha made them command the respect of everyone in the village. These elders now taught the young men how to fish, build canoes, and fight battles. It was said that some of the white-haired men who sat outside the huts across from Mrs. McBeal's mission school were over one hundred years old.

They were the authorities of the land, even above the Chief. But on this day, the Chief decided to exercise his own authority over the village.

Eugene, Oliver, and Mrs. McBeal were standing on the *lanai* of the mission school when they witnessed the Chief yelling in anger, his face turning red and his cheeks puffing out like two balloons.

"What's goin' on?" asked Reverend McBeal when he arrived.

"Seems the *taro* fields that were harvested got planted last night," replied Mrs. McBeal, "along with another bridge built!"

When Lucy, Elizabeth, and the Bishop entered the village a little later, they were frightened by the chaos in the street. Young and old people were running in all directions.

"Why aren't the islanders on the building site?" What's happening here?" asked the Bishop when they joined up with the rest of the McBeals.

"I'm not sure,' replied the Reverend. "But we need ter get ter the bottom of this, and right now."

"Lucy, it is not safe here. Go and hide with Maile," ordered her father.

"Yes, Papa." Lucy tried to make her way through the crowd. She couldn't believe her eyes. The young men seemed to be trying to protect the older men as they were herded by Burles toward their Chief. Suddenly, Kalani and his friends turned and formed a wall between the older islanders and Burles.

Burles' horse reared as the men attempted to surround Burles. He turned to escape into the forest, shouting out, "This settlement will get finished on time or you will all pay!"

Frightened by the massive crowd, Lucy made her way to Maile's hut, sneaking behind the huts.

When she entered, Lucy heard someone say, *"He mai, noho malie."* It was *Hoku.* He sat calmly on a *lau hala* mat at the center of the room with his hands raised high into the air. He began whispering a chant.

"He wants you to come, sit quietly," translated Maile.

"But my father is out there, I just can't sit quietly," Lucy said turning around and peeking through the doorway.

"You can stop all this," said Hoku.

The little girl came over and sat down next to them. "Maile, what is he talking about?"

"Lucy Tuppins, you have had the power all along," explained Maile.

"It I had powers, don't you think I would use them to save your people?" Lucy asked in frustration, tears filling her eyes. "Even the *Menehune* had to help me when I was in trouble."

"'*Ae*," acknowledged *Hoku*, nodding. "I know of this."

"What do you mean, you know?" asked Lucy. "No one else was there."

"He sees what others do not. He says that they protect you, watch over you. Remember the storm? The fire pit and the stones?" asked Maile.

Lucy sat there baffled. "But why me? *Hoku*, I don't even know how I could help."

Hoku took Lucy's tiny hands into his, and she felt peace flow through her arm and into her heart. The old healer looked into her eyes with a piercing gaze.

"You are the key. Trust the *Menehune*, they will show you. Now, go," he instructed.

"Into the forest?" Lucy asked.

Hoku nodded. "Yes. Follow the path to the waterfall. You will find the guide that you seek."

"You remember the way, don't you?" questioned Maile.

"Yes," said Lucy, slumping and sulking at the very idea of going into the forest by herself and crossing the stream alone.

"Let your heart lead you. You have a special strength. It is the power that will straighten all the trouble out," said Maile.

At that moment, Eugene and Oliver came running into the hut.

"Whew!" exclaimed Oliver. "It is a crazy out there."

"Aye," agreed Eugene.

Hoku stood up and revealed a back exit behind a drape. "Go. Now!"

"Go? Where?" asked Eugene.

"You ask too many questions, Eugene. Just follow me," said Lucy.

The children sneaked around Maile's hut, making sure that the coast was clear before running toward the edge of the forest.

Thirty-One

Kidnapped

Elizabeth couldn't find her brothers. She searched for them throughout the village but there was no sign of them. She wondered if they had gone into the forest for safety and hustled into the trees.

"Oliver!" she called out. "Eugene!"

Suddenly she felt a tug around her waist. She spun around. To her surprise, it was Reverend Machesney.

"Don' worry. I'll protect yeh," he said, pulling her closer.

"I don' need protectin'!" Elizabeth insisted, pushing his hands away.

"Oh, but yeh do." Reverend Machesney backed her against a tree trunk, grabbed her forearms, and kissed her hard.

"Ugh!" She wrinkled her nose in disgust and spit in his face.

"Yeh shouldn' have done that," he warned wiping the spit from his cheek. Elizabeth glared defiantly at the clergyman before he spun her around and bound her wrists together. "I want ter take care of yeh," he whispered maliciously in her ear.

"Let me go," demanded Elizabeth struggling to get free. "Help!" she shouted.

"I see that yeh are goin' ter be a handful," Reverend Machesney said playfully. He took a handkerchief and tied it around her mouth. Then he swung her petite body over his shoulder and walked deeper into the jungle, carrying the helpless young woman.

The three children were very careful not to slip as they climbed down into the ravine. Lucy made it to the *noni* bushes first. She wasn't surprised that their branches were stripped clean from the rushing water earlier in the week.

"Isn' this where yeh almost drowned, Lucy?" asked Oliver, throwing a stone into the narrow stream of water.

"Yes. Now, if only I could remember where the cave entrance is," replied Lucy.

Lucy waded down the gulch, moving debri of uprooted bushes and broken tree limbs out of her way. A bright light glistened deep in the thicket. She reached further into the brush and saw her locket dangling from a twig.

"Look! My locket, I found it!" Lucy quickly snatched it up, then stuffed it in her purse.

Irritated, Eugene asked, "Did yeh drag us out here just fer that?"

"No. We're looking for the entrance to a cave. Do you see an overhang . . . " Lucy said, hoisting herself onto a ledge. "I know it's around here, somewhere." Long tree roots dangled down along the face of the rocks. Lucy slowly stepped, searching through the roots for an entrance.

Oliver kept close behind her and pulled himself up over the boulders to the ledge. Eugene tagged along below, getting more bored by the minute and rested on a large boulder in the gulch. He watched his brother climb up on the ledge to join Lucy. Above his head a large shadow blocked out the sunlight, and as he looked up he saw a huge bird sailing towards Lucy and Oliver. "Lucy!" he shouted. "Look out!"

The albatross gracefully soared down and landed on the ledge next to the younger children. Oliver froze in his tracks. He was so stunned that when he tried to say something, it just came out as gibberish.

"Hello again," Lucy greeted the bird and curtsied. "Is this the right place?" The bird nodded then flew away.

"Never seen anythin' like it," mumbled Oliver. Then, regaining his wits, he turned in amazement to his friend. "Lucy Tuppins, yeh spoke to it! An albatross! There is somethin' different about that brain of yehrs."

Lucy called down to Eugene. 'Hurry up. This is the place!"

Eugene didn't want to be left alone with a giant bird nearby, so he scrambled up the rocks, slipping and sliding all the way. "Where's Oliver?" he asked when he reached the ledge.

Lucy pulled back the long roots covering the cave's entrance. "Oh, he's in here," she said pointing.

The tunnel ahead of them grew darker as it went deeper. But that wouldn't stop Lucy from looking for the *Menehune*. She pressed on, the two boys in tow.

"Will someone please tell me why we're in this awful place?" Eugene pleaded.

"I've got to find the Menehune," Lucy replied.

"Ha! Sure yeh do," Eugene scoffed.

"No, she's tellin' the truth," insisted Oliver as he led them deeper into the tunnel along the narrow walls. The boy knew that the tubes joined to form corridors that connected underground caves.

"Good Lord, I can' believe yeh led us on this wild goose chase," signed Eugene. Then he let out a shrill scream as his hand slipped on something cold and slimy.

"Come on, will yeh? Quit goofing around," urged Oliver.

Along a dark ledge Oliver pulled himself forward, securing his fingers in holes in the wall. He could feel parts of the wall crumbling under the weight of his hands. Then something fell to the ground.

"What was that?" he asked looking at the round object between his feet.

Lucy moved forward and slowly squatted behind Oliver. In the darkness, she ran her fingers along the object and realized that it was a skull. She lifted it up for a better look.

Oliver took one look at it and screamed with fright.

Lucy huffed and shook her head. "You two have no sense for adventure," she said, dropping the skull and proceeding hand over hand around Oliver.

"I don't like it here," cried Oliver, holding onto the back of her dress for guidance.

"Me neither. Creepy, if yeh ask me," agreed Eugene, with a crack in his voice.

"I know where we are!" Lucy announced.

Oliver and Eugene looked at each other with uncertainty.

"Eugene, do yeh suppose we're goin' ter be damned ter hell for disturbin' these bones?" Oliver continued to cry.

The boys were shaking in their shoes. It was cold and musty in the tunnel, and they were frightened.

Eugene reached forward and tugged at Oliver's shoulder. "Oliver, let's get out of here."

Oliver let go of Lucy's dress and the two boys started backtracking to the cave's entrance.

Lucy turned around and stood there with her hands on her hips. "What a couple of brave Scottish gents you both turned out to be," she called in angry disgust.

"Courage has nothin' ter do with it," argued Eugene. "Good Lord Lucy. These are dead people!"

Oliver wanted to be brave, and most of all he wanted Lucy to think of him as her equal. Stepping away from Eugene, he started along the ledge toward Lucy when he tripped and fell face down on two skulls. This time both boys screamed at the horror of impending death.

"Get a hold of yourselves," admonished Lucy, bending down to help Oliver back to his feet. "They've been here for centuries, and will probably be here for a lot longer if you two quit knocking them down." She noticed a long trail of evenly placed stones beneath Oliver's feet and looked closer. "Oliver, what are these?"

"Menehune!" he exclaimed.

"I knew I was in the right place," she announced excitedly.

"Look, Eugene!" said Oliver, standing up and wiping away his tears. "They lead in there." The young boy pointed past Lucy to a faint light at the end of the ledge.

"I've been here before. Just follow the trail of stones," commanded Lucy.

"Told yeh," said Oliver, smirking at Eugene. "They are real."

Thirty-Two

The Treasure

Into a huge cavern the children walked. The ceiling was at least thirty feet above their heads, and was covered in a web of brown tree roots. Lucy looked up and remembered when she was there once before. "This is it," she whispered. Rays of light coming through small holes in the ceiling illuminated a stream in the distance.

"How long do yeh think this has been here?," asked Oliver.

"Probably thousands of years," remarked Eugene looking around at the vastness of the cave.

Lucy noticed dark patches in the walls, which turned out to be shadows of tunnels that branched off of the main cavern. Water originating from one of those openings flowed rapidly across the bumpy ground, emptying out over a ledge into the lower level of the cave.

"Blimey, this would make a grand fort," said Oliver, treading across the six foot wide stream and up onto a huge boulder. Back and forth he parried an imaginary sword. "And I'm the defender of the loot."

Eventually, Eugene lost his fear and crossed the stream too. He and Oliver ran further into the cave from one alcove to the next, exploring the tiny rooms around sides of the cavern.

Meanwhile, Lucy decided to stay behind and explore the side of the cave she was in. She disappeared into a dark crevasse, but not for very long.

Screams suddenly rang throughout the cave, startling Lucy. She was peering out of the tunnel when she heard a deep voice echoing from the other end of the cavern. The silhouette of a large man in a hooded cape appeared in the distance. *It couldn't be! Is it the same man I met months ago in the dark alley? The man who killed the Queen's guard?*

His six foot body stood tall and mighty some two hundred feet away from where Lucy was hiding. She watched him lift Oliver and Eugene high in the air by their belts.

"Just knew yeh kids would spoil all my plans," growled the man.

"Spoil?" asked Oliver indignantly.

"He means that we've ruined his plans," clarified Eugene.

The man carried the two boys over the rocks to the lower level of the cavern. He trapped Oliver face down on the ground beneath his boot while tying up Eugene. While his hands and feet were bound, his mouth gagged, and his eyes blindfolded, the older boy didn't put up a struggle. Oliver in contrast, squirmed with his whole body and tried to backwards kick the man in the leg. His captor merely increased the pressure of the boot on his back, crushing the air out of the boy's lungs. Soon Oliver was trussed up just like his brother.

Lucy didn't know what to do. She didn't want to get caught too. The air in the cave was getting colder and a dampness settled on Lucy like an unwanted shawl. But she didn't dare step into the light and risk being seen.

Then out of nowhere, another figure appeared. She watched as he climbed down from a hole in the cave's ceiling. It was the same hole where Lucy had escaped a week before. He approached the hooded man on the ledge. He looked familiar, but Lucy could only see his back.

"What in blazes are yeh doin' here?" asked the hooded man.

"I've been following you for some time," the newcomer replied.

Then Lucy recognized the second man's voice; it was Burles. She was confused. *If the hooded man isn't Burles, then who is he?*

Curiosity got the better of her. Lucy suppressed her fears and slid out from behind a large boulder to crouch down near the stream's edge for a better look.

Burles struck with all his might a sharp blow to the hooded man's head. "You stole that money," he said furiously, hitting the man again. "That was my father they sent to jail for your crime." The hooded man stumbled back a little and shook off the punches.

"The boat fer Tahiti leaves tonight, and I'll be long gone before anyone can figure it out," he gloated as he pulled out a gun.

Lucy heard the sound of a gunshot ricocheting through-out the cave and watched Burles' body fall to the ground.

"You'll never get away with it," Burles threatened feebly as the man tied him up. Then Burles' head dropped forward and he was unconscious.

Lucy's eyes followed the man's movements as he dragged a bulging satchel out of one of the alcoves. He lumbered up from the lower level through a narrow passage. When he finally reached the ceiling level, he exited out the hole.

As soon as he was out of sight, Lucy stood up and faced the stream flowing alongside her feet. She knew that if she slipped, the water would carry her down over the ledge possibly drop her to her death.

So she moved slowly into the water, with one foot in front of the other as Kalani had told her before. Each step made her heart race faster, but she was determined to do this. When she looked to the lower ledge and saw Eugene and Oliver struggling against their restraints, she realized she was going too slowly and there was no time to waste.

"I've got to do this," Lucy whispered to herself, over and over taking in a deep breath and forcing herself to walk faster across the cold flowing water. She hoped that she still had that protective energy shield around her that *Hoku* told her about.

All of a sudden her foot slipped off a stone and Lucy teetered back and forth trying to regain her balance. But all her efforts couldn't stop her fall and she went down into the water with a splash.

Soaking wet and breathing hard, Lucy stood up and searched for a way to climb down to the boys. She found small hand and foot holds just her size in the ledge wall and hurried down them.

First, she removed Eugene's blindfold. He was still gagged and couldn't say anything, but he kicked his legs frantically and kept looking desperately back and forth from her eyes to above her head. Lucy tried to untie his legs since she thought that's what he wanted.

"Really, Eugene! It's me, calm down," she whispered. "You never were one with any patience. Blasts! Just hold still, will you?"

It was then that Lucy felt something latch on to her shoulder. Within the blink of an eye, the hooded man had grabbed Lucy and lifted her into the air, digging his fingers into her skin.

Lucy looked down into a pair of blue eyes and then she and recognized the red hair curling around the dark hood. "You!" she cried out.

"Lucy Tuppins," said Reverend Machesney maliciously, "Yeh've been a pain in my side fer months. Yeh don' remember that night in London, do yeh?"

"Put me down!" she demanded.

The clergyman narrowed his eyes. "I should have run yeh over in that alley when I had the chance."

Lucy's flailing made her leather purse slip off her shoulder and down over his arm. She immediately stopped squirming and stared at it. Reverend Machesney dropped her to the ground, pinned her under his foot, and opened the purse.

"I saw you murder that sentry," she spat out, struggling against his boot.

The clergyman emptied the gem, coin, and ring into the palm of his hand and grunted. He threw the ring at Burles' unconscious body and put the others in his pocket. "Well, yeh're not goin' ter live long enough ter tell anyone, are yeh?" he said, grinning wickedly.

"But you can't kill me," Lucy argued. 'You'll have the blood of two on your hands if you do."

"So?" Reverend Machesney scoffed at her.

Lucy turned her head to glare at the clergyman out of the corner of her eyes. "God doesn't let murderers into heaven, I'm sure of that!"

Reverend Machesney had heard enough of the girl's idle threats and quickly silenced her by gagging her mouth and binding her arms and legs. He also retied Eugene's blind-fold and checked to make sure all the others' bindings were secure.

"The river should be rising soon; and by the time they find yehr bodies, I'll be gone with my treasures." He turned away and made his escape out of the cave.

Lucy sat helpless in the dirt. To her left were Eugene and Oliver, tied up just like she was. To her right was Burles, bleeding and unconscious. The tears welled up in her eyes as she faced the fact that she'd failed the boys and *Hoku*.

After all, her mission had been to find the *Menehune* and help the islanders. But there she was, stranded and unable to help anyone. All thoughts of being strong and courageous disappeared as the exhausted little girl cried herself to sleep.

Thiry-Three

The Earthquake

Kalani and *Hoku* were standing on the hill overlooking the building spot when they felt the earth shake underneath their feet. No once, but twice.

In the distance, they saw trees near the Bishop's white house fall, crashing to the ground with the second tremor. Kalani felt the third tremor shake. Then he saw the workers jump from the bridge construction and scurry back to their village for safety.

"Look!" shouted *Hoku*, pointing to boulders rolling down the mountainside. They crushed everything in their path. It was a disastrous sight.

The two men made their way down a path and found a heap of rubble at the bottom. To their surprise, they also found Bishop Tuppins. He stood frozen in place with a blank stare on his face. *Hoku* reached out to touch him when an aftershock rumbled beneath them. When they all looked at each other, Kalani and *Hoku* could see the terror clearly in the Bishop's eyes.

Dust got kicked up into the air from workers scrambling everywhere. In the commotion, the Bishop was pushed to the ground.

Hoku and Kalani ran to his aid, and reached down together to pull him up.

"The children!" Have you seen the children?" the Bishop cried out. He grabbed the leaf lei that hung around *Hoku*'s neck, and pleaded. "I don't know what to do!"

"We'll help you find them, don't worry," assured Kalani.

Meanwhile back in the cave, the tremors woke Lucy out of a sound sleep. For a groggy moment, she thought it was all a bad dream. But then she realized she was still tied up and the cave shuddered again. Within seconds, rocks broke free from their places on the ceiling and walls. She looked over at the boys, and then felt the cold splash of water on her face as a rock fell nearby. The water was rising.

Just as she was about to panic, Lucy felt stubby fingers reach around her head and untie the gag. Then her hands were untied. She thought it was Kalani, but it wasn't.

A little man walked out from behind her. He looked like a leprechaun, but was wearing a lot less clothing. His skin was a deep shade of brown, and his body reminded her of an over-stuffed teddy bear. She laughed when she saw his round belly and fuzzy black hair. He stood there blinking his eyes at her.

"I knew you'd come!" she exclaimed untying her feet.

A mixed feeling of joy and wonderment filled her. Lining the upper level of the cave, just inside the shadows, was an army of miniature warriors. Lucy spun around and laughed. She counted thirty more *Menehune* smiling back at her.

"Fantastic!" she shouted, bouncing with delight. She was so happy that she almost forgot about the danger she was in.

"*Hoku* says that you build the bridges each night," Lucy said, stepping out of the water.

The little men all nodded in unison. She giggled at the sight and then one of them approached her, resting his hands on his hips. She wondered if he was their leader and addressed him directly.

"You have to stop. Oh, I don't mean that you've done a bad thing; it's just that it's making matters worse in the village," she explained.

The little man turned to leave, and Lucy suddenly worried that she had failed to communicate with them.

"Wait. Don't go," she pleaded, grabbing his arm. "I don't know what I'm supposed to do." She didn't understand why these little men didn't talk to her. Maybe they couldn't speak? She tried talking to the leader again.

"Burles – the big *haole* man! He's over there, and I don't think he'll be hurting anyone again so you don't have to keep destroying the bridge at night." The *Menehune* leader only blinked and continued to stare at her. "Do you understand what I'm saying?" she asked, pulling the twigs out of her skirt. The little man nodded and Lucy sighed.

"Well, that's a relief! Now there's the matter of the Queen's treasure."

At this point, Eugene and Oliver were squirming uncontrollably. They could hear every word Lucy was saying, but because of their blindfolds, they couldn't see a thing.

"*Hoku* says that you can help me. Please, you've just got to," the little girl pleaded.

Out of the corner of her eye, Lucy saw something move on the far cave wall. There was a heavy thud followed by a scraping rumble noise. Then she saw a huge boulder rolling towards the ledge, heading right for them. Lucy couldn't believe what happened next. The little army of men rallied together and blocked the boulder with their unified strength, turning it aside with ease.

Remembering her friends, Lucy went over to Eugene and Oliver and began untying them. As soon as Oliver's hands were free, he tore off his blindfold.

"Where are they?" he demanded. "Lucy Tuppins! I know yeh were talkin' ter the *Menehune*."

"Oliver, they're right over – ," she turned and was about to point when she saw that the little men had left.

"Saints alive, lassie, what took yeh so long ter untie me?" he scolded.

As soon as Eugene was free he stood up and grabbed Oliver by the arm. "No time ter be lookin' fer *Menehune*," he said urgently, pulling his little brother away from the rising water.

A swarm of large roaches trying to escape the cave crawled up Eugene's pant leg. "Centipedes!" he shouted, stomping his foot.

"Roaches; only roaches, Eugene," corrected Oliver calmly, helping his brother swat them off.

The trio pulled Burles' body away from the rising water. Unconscious and still tied up, the man was of no danger to the children.

Suddenly, he opened his eyes. The trio jumped backwards in surprise.

"Untie me!" Burles shouted.

"Now why would I want to do that?" Lucy asked.

"He's getting away, that's why," Burles said looking up at the hole in the ceiling. "He must be stopped."

Lucy hesitated a moment. "Oh, and you are going to drag yourself through the jungles after him with only one good leg?" she asked pointing to the blood oozing out of his thigh.

Burles' face winced at the pain. "Yes, if I have to. Now I command you to untie me this instant!"

"I don't think so. You can wait here until we figure out what to do with you," said Lucy. She turned to Oliver and Eugene. "What we need to do is go get the Queen's treasure from Reverend Machesney. Come on boys."

"You can't just leave me here to drown! What if the river rises higher?" Burles yelled struggling against his restraints.

Lucy spun around and looked him straight in the eyes. She actually felt sorry for him. "You know, Reverend Machesney had me fooled. I thought that you were the thief."

"And why would I want to steal from the Queen?" he replied indignantly.

Lucy frowned at Burles. 'You have to admit, you are not a very kind person."

"All I wanted to do is get out of London and have my own life. I was sick and tired of having to be polite and follow all the rules at the Palace," he explained looking away. "I thought that after I got finished with the job here, I'd move onto India and buy some land. I certainly didn't expect to get tangled up with the crime of the century way out here in the Pacific Ocean."

"Your father will be pardoned as soon as Reverend Machesney is caught," promised Lucy. "Don't you want to be there when that happens? You've done enough damage here." She wasn't afraid of him any longer. He was just a lost soul who needed a chance to right his ways.

"I'm really sorry for all the trouble I've caused, honest," he admitted. "Will you just untie me now?"

"Don' trust him, Lucy," cautioned Eugene.

"Believe me," Burles pleaded. "I know where Machesney is headed. I can help you.

"All right," said Lucy, reluctantly. "But don't make me regret this." She bent down and untied Burles.

"Just great!" grumbled Eugene, shaking his head.

"Follow me," commanded Burles. "He's headed for the ship that leaves for Tahiti tonight."

Thirty-Four

A GUNSHOT

Oliver held his compass tightly in the palm of his hand. "This way!" he shouted, leading them onward through the thicket of the forest. He had convinced them that they would make better time if they stayed off the path and cut straight through the trees.

"Stop!" he cried out suddenly, staring intently at the instrument in his hand.

"There's no time, Oliver," gasped Lucy.

"I knew we'd get lost. Told yeh that we should stick ter the path," said Eugene, panting.

"We are not lost," grumbled Oliver.

Burles sat down on a stump to rest. He had lost a lot of blood and was feeling faint. They all stood around him, trying to breathe long calm breaths of air.

Lucy bent down at her waist, holding her sides in pain. "Which way, Oliver?"

Oliver held up his compass for a better look and pointed. "West. Yes, I'm sure of it," he declared, running in the direction of west.

"Alright then," sighed Eugene, running after his brother.

"I've got to rest a moment longer," breathed Burles.

"Oliver and Eugene," Lucy called out. "We'll catch up later. Tell our fathers to get down to the docks with the Chief and stop that boat from leaving."

The boys stopped and turned around looking at Lucy in confusion.

"Yes, go!" she waved them away.

Oliver and Eugene took off running and were out of sight within minutes.

Burles slumped to the ground. His face was pale.

"You don't look too good," remarked Lucy.

"I just need to rest a little, that's all."

"Tell me," she asked, "Did you really think that your father robbed the Queen?"

He gave her a skeptical look. "Him? No! My father is the kindest and most honest man I've ever known and he adores the Queen. He's been in her service for over forty years."

Lucy questioned him further. "Then why didn't you stay in London when they took him to jail?"

"Well, we don't exactly see eye to eye. He didn't want me to go to India," Burles replied.

"I bet he would rather you be near him. It was you who risked your life for his innocence back in the cave." Lucy game him an encouraging smile.

"There was just something odd about that clergyman always hanging around the construction site and then disappearing for long periods of time. So one day I decided to follow him. Didn't know about the loot he'd hidden, but I knew he was up to something in that cave," explained Burles.

"Mr. Burles," Lucy interrupted, "I think we'd better get going now."

Burles nodded and then pointed. "Would you mind handing me that dead branch over there? It will make a good walking stick."

Lucy pushed through the brush and was making her way over to the branch when she saw something sparkle on the ground. She bent down and retrieved three objects. Quickly Lucy stood up and held them high into the air, waving at Burles with her free hand. "He went this way!"

"What do you have there?" asked Burles.

"Two coins," she answered. "But this is Elizabeth's hair comb. What would it be doing out here unless Reverend Machesney has taken her?"

Unknowingly, she and Burles had wandered in a different direction than the boys had taken out of the forest. But luckily, it was the direction the thief had taken. Up ahead Lucy spotted Reverend Machesney pacing in front of a huge tree.

"Shhhh," she whispered, pointing to the tree. "Look! And there's Elizabeth."

Burles limped along and Lucy crept closer. Her thoughts were busy in her head trying to figure out a way to catch the thief without putting Elizabeth in danger.

"I'll create a distraction," she explained.

But Burles wanted revenge and he was itching for a fight with the clergyman. "Let me at him," he growled.

Lucy grabbed at his sleeve. "Wait. Reverend Machesney probably has a few more bullets in that gun of his. You run at him and he'll just shoot you dead this time."

Burles calmed his rage and considered for a moment. "So, what do you propose we do?" he asked.

Lucy pointed. "I'm going to climb that tree. You'll know what to do when the time is right."

She snuck over, hiding behind the massive tree trunk and climbed up, masterly as high as she could reach.

Meanwhile, Reverend Machesney stopped his pacing and bent down to talk to Elizabeth. She was gagged and bound, sitting against the trunk of a tree with tears rolling down her cheeks.

"Don't cry," he crooned, stroking her hair with his fingers.

When the clergyman leaned forward and gently placed a kiss on Elizabeth's forehead, Lucy let out an awful cry like the sound of a monkey's scream. It startled Reverend Machesney and he spun around, looking up frantically into the trees to find the creature it came from.

The moment had come for Burles to seize the chance by attacking the Reverend. He jumped out from behind a bush and hurled himself at the clergyman. They fought each other violently; punching, and shoving, and kicking.

Elizabeth, still bound and gagged, lifted her eyes and saw Lucy straddling a branch.

"Hi!" called the little girl, waving down to her friend.

Then there was the sound of a gunshot.

Lucy looked towards the beach through the tree's branches and saw Kalani approaching with a group of islanders. And that was the last thing she saw before she fell to the ground, feeling a stabbing pain ripple through her body.

Thirty-Five

Keiki with Hair like the Sun

B ishop Tuppins held Lucy in his arms at the base of the big tree. Her tiny limbs hung lifeless as he pleaded to God. He wasn't making any sense as he randomly shouted out various bible verses he'd memorized.

"Bishop, sir," consoled Elizabeth, placing her delicate hand on his shoulder. "The Lord hears yehr prayers and he won' let her die. I'm sure of that!"

"She's all I have," he blubbered through his tears.

"Then let us help," insisted Kalani. He pulled Lucy away from her father's embrace and gathered the little girl into his arms.

There were no doctors or hospitals on the island. But *Hoku*, the healer, and his island medicine was much better. The islanders put their trust in him for decades. The Bishop had no choice but to let the healer care for his daughter.

Hundreds of islanders gathered around. The big white house was surrounded by them, a vigil for the *keiki* who lay inside.

Reverend and Mrs. McBeal sat outside on the lanai, holding hands and praying for Lucy. All who came that afternoon shared in their tears. There wasn't much anyone could do but pray for Lucy, so people held hands and said the Lord's Prayer many times.

"That bullet was meant for me," murmured Burles. He placed a bouquet of flowers by the front door. "She's a very brave little girl."

Maile led the island children around the outside of the house, placing colorful flowered *leis* on the railings and window sills.

Even the Chief was there.

His tall body was frightening to most, but on this day he came humbly to the front steps of the house with concern in his heart for the *keiki* with hair like the sun. "Mrs. McBeal," he asked. "How is the little one?"

Mrs. McBeal looked up with tears in her eyes. She couldn't bring herself to say anything through the sadness.

Maile approached and placed a lei around her neck. She turned to the Chief and reassured him by saying, "We are all prayin' fer Lucy and she'll be fine, we just know it!"

The Chief nodded. He had never seen his people gather with such passion for prayer. He stood and watched them in wonderment, finally stepping down and joining the group.

Inside the house, Oliver and Eugene prayed with the Bishop in the study. While on the dining room table across the hall, Lucy lay outstretched, her body motionless on the slab of *koa* wood, tended by Elizabeth, Kalani, and *Hoku*.

"Oh, Kalani," sobbed Elizabeth, "I don' know what ter do." Tears threatened to flow down her rosy cheeks.

"Bring the Bishop here," he told her.

"But he does not believe there is any hope," she said.

Hoku took her face in his hands and insisted, "The father should be here."

Elizabeth left the dining room in search of Lucy's father.

Moments later, she returned with the Bishop, who was angry.

"All the dark medicine you people practice is not going to help my little girl," he shouted, clenching his bible under his arm.

Elizabeth felt sorry for the Bishop. His voice was angry, but she knew that his heart was breaking from sadness. She took his hand and pressed it against Lucy's heart and said, "She is not goin' ter die; not here, not now."

Suddenly he realized that Lucy was not moving. He took her by the shoulders and shook her tiny body. "Wake up, dear child. Please wake up!"

Slowly Elizabeth reached down and guided his hands away from Lucy. "Come with me. We need fer yeh ter help us now."

The Bishop stood with Elizabeth along the wall. They both sighed, holding each other's hands, and watched as *Hoku* and Kalani placed brightly green and red colored *ti* leaves around the edge of the table.

But the Bishop was impatient and when Kalani and *Hoku* began chanting in unison, he yanked his hand free from Elizabeth and shook his finger at her. He demanded, "I don't need them here with their chants and superstitions."

She took in a deep breath and mustered up the strong Scottish character that she kept hidden from most people. Elizabeth reached up for his pointing finger and firmly announced, "We're livin' in a jungle, if yeh've not noticed. There's no doctor. There's no English medicine. All we have is our faith and the love of the island people. So, please get a hold of yerself!"

The Bishop was surprised at Elizabeth's outburst. But it was just exactly what he needed to bring him to his senses and let go of his anger.

Before the Bishop could respond, Leah entered the room from the kitchen, carrying wooden bowls full of *poi*. *Hoku* offered one to the Bishop while Elizabeth and Kalani each took one for themselves. *Hoku* explained, "We will show her the *aloha* in this room."

"Are you daft? You're going to eat now?" asked the Bishop with disbelief, placing the bowl on a nearby table. His anger was flaring up again as he grew impatient with the healer. His nostrils flared as he reached under his arm for the bible. "Rubbish," he muttered while leafing through the pages, trying to find the appropriate verse to pray with.

Hoku looked at the clergyman. He could feel the loss that still tormented Lucy's father. There was no passion; what stood before him was only the shadow of a desperate man consumed by bitterness and hatred.

"There," Hoku said, setting the last bowl down on the table. "For the gods."

"MY God listens, not eats!" shouted the Bishop.

Lifting the Bishop's bowl, *Hoku* shoved it toward the Bishop's face and offered, "For you. Eat now."

Kalani noticed that the Bishop was confused, so he explained, "It is our custom to offer up to the spirit in the room a bowl of *poi*. It is out of respect that we also eat."

The three of them ate from the bowls, scooping up the soft mashed purple root with their fingers. As they were eating, the harmonious sounds of children singing rang from outside the window and the Bishop felt the tension that gripped every muscle in his body fade away.

After they finished eating, the healer placed his hands on Lucy's forehead and closed his eyes in concentration for a moment. Then he instructed the Bishop, "It is Lucy that you should be holding and not your book. Put it down and tell her of the *aloha* you feel for her. She needs to know that you love her, she needs to feel it through your touch."

It had been a long time since the Bishop had let his heart bear the sadness he had pushed away when his wife died. He was alone now, and he was scared. Had he forgotten the true meaning of love? He tried to remember the last time he read a story to Lucy at night, held her tight, or kissed her goodnight. *Hoku's* words brought Bishop Tuppins to tears.

The bible was placed on the table and the Bishop sobbed as he lifted Lucy's frail body into his arms. The prayer that came to his lips this time was not from verses on printed paper, but from the deepest part of his soul.

"Oh merciful Lord, please forgive me. Don't take this precious child from me."

Kalani and Elizabeth placed their hands on his shoulders in support.

The Bishop continued, "I couldn't endure life without her and I know now that I've been selfish with my time. I'm so sorry. Please, just give me another chance to be a good father." He turned his gaze to the heavens and begged God silently with all his being.

Elizabeth began to lose hope and cried sadly. Kalani held her tightly to him and stroked her hair.

It was *Hoku* who saw Lucy open her eyes. He smiled at the little *keiki* and she smiled weakly back.

"Papa?" whispered Lucy.

Bishop Tuppins opened his eyes at the sound of his daughter's voice. "Yes, yes," he replied, smothering her in a hug. "You are going to be okay."

Elizabeth pushed free of Kalani's embrace and took Lucy's little hand in hers. "Yeh gave us quite a scare, little lassie," she announced.

Lucy's father whispered into her ear, "I love you very much, sweet princess."

"Aye, love. It is truly the greatest gift. Faith and hope are important, too. But love is the most powerful. After all, didn' the good Lord mean fer us ter share this gift with all our hearts?" commented Elizabeth.

The Bishop looked across the table at the old healer. He knew that he could never fully thank *Hoku* for saving his daughter's life.

"You've opened up my eyes to the wisdom and power you and your people have known to survive here on this island. And I'm so thankful that God has blessed me and Lucy with your friendship."

Hoku smiled. He knew the Bishop had much to learn about the Hawaiian way of life and he was glad the clergyman found his way back to loving his little girl.

Lucy's father took a step backwards, bowing before Kalani, Elizabeth, and Hoku, he said with a twinkle of joy in his eyes, "Mahalo for everything and not giving up on me."

Thirty-Six

The Invitation

January 1827

It had been months since Lucy had fallen from the tree. She had settled into a much quieter routine and prided herself in being the best pupil in her small class of three.

As for Eugene, he finally decided that Lucy wasn't all that troublesome. After all, he only had to put up with her for three more months and he'd be off to England for his advanced studies. But until then, he secretly hoped that Lucy's active imagination would lead them on some more adventures before his departure.

Oliver was delighted that someone else besides him held the secrets of the *Menehune* deep down inside their soul. He and Lucy shared a special bond that was rooted in those secrets. Every night they perched themselves on the branches of the big tree, recalling their adventures.

Elizabeth and Kalani continued to meet in secret behind the canoe hut in the village. However, it was no secret among the islanders that Elizabeth had stolen Kalani's heart, and that they were destined to be together.

The Bishop and the Chief had found a way to work together so that the settlement buildings all got built, and the *taro* fields were saved.

And as for the *Menehune*, they continued to slip into the new settlement each night and eventually build a system of walls and bridges. Once again, the stream brought water down from the mountainside to the people and their plants.

Lucy hadn't seen the little brown men since that night when Reverend Machesney was arrested, but she sensed their presence during her walks in the forest. She had hoped there would come a time when she'd see their funny little faces again.

The Bishop and Reverend McBeal were very proud of the new settlement, and looked forward to the third company arriving from England.

A new house rested within walking distance of the church. It was different from the white clapboard house with its long *lanai*. This structure was made of precisely cut rock. Its majestic, high-vaulted ceiling spanned the entire ground floor. Lucy was going to miss climbing out her bedroom window onto the big tree. But, her bedroom in the new stone house had one enticing special feature: a long bookcase to house her insect jar collection. She couldn't wait to move in.

"It's not goin' ter be the same, yeh bein' down the road, I mean," sighed Elizabeth, sitting next to Lucy on the edge of the little girl's bed.

"I'm going to miss you, too," Lucy replied, hugging Elizabeth.

The sound of heavy footsteps running up the staircase towards Lucy's room could only mean that Oliver and Eugene had exciting news they wanted to share.

The door burst open with the two boys squeezing through the opening together. Oliver held up a piece of paper in his hand and shouted, "Got a letter, I have!"

"Oliver McBeal," scolded his sister, "Now where are yehr manners?"

Oliver didn't care about manners at that moment because he had something exciting to share with them. He jumped up onto the mattress next to the girls, waving the small white paper in front of Lucy. "It's got a seal on the back. See? I didn' open it."

"Who is it fer?" asked Elizabeth, grabbing the flapping envelope.

"Why Lucy, of course," he replied, snatching it back.

Oliver handed it to Lucy and she raised it to her nose. It smelled of a sweet fragrance. She traced the lines of the raised waxed seal with her fingers.

"That's the royal seal!" blurted out Elizabeth. "And why would a lassie like yeh be receivin' such an important letter?" She grabbed it out of Lucy's hand to look at it up close.

"Probably should have been sent ter Eugene," mused Oliver. "He's headed fer that fancy school in London."

"A school didn' send this," remarked Elizabeth.

"Hey, it's addressed to me," Lucy insisted, swiping it back.

The four sat on the mattress staring down at the paper. It was an unusual sight for anyone on the island to receive parcels or envelopes, since they had to come a long way by sea. They all sucked in a breath of hesitation when Lucy tore open the envelope, breaking the seal.

"Well, read it," urged Oliver.

"Hold on, she's takin' her time. It's no ordinary letter, yeh know!" said Elizabeth.

Lucy held the small card in her hand and read the message:

To My Dear Lucy Tuppins,

I understand that you exposed the thief who stole my jewels. You are a very brave young girl. I wish you to come visit me when you are next in London. We have much to discuss. Bring this letter with you, and you will be granted an audience. Gratefully yours, THE QUEEN

"No!" exclaimed Elizabeth. "I don' believe it."

"When are yeh goin'?" asked Oliver, jumping up and down on the mattress.

Lucy shook her head at her friend. "It's not like I can just jump on a boat and go anytime I want."

"Yeh could go with Mam and Eugene when he travels fer his private schoolin' this fall," suggested Elizabeth.

Lucy's eyes lit up at that idea. "Maybe I could."

"The Queen, Lucy. Just imagine that. Yeh're goin' ter see the Queen!" said Oliver.

"Yes, I think I am," grinned Lucy holding the letter close to her heart.

Hawaiian Word's Dictionary

ʻaina	the land
aliʻi	descended from Kings & Queens
aloha	hello, love, good-bye
guava	a round yellow-skinned fruit with a sweet pink pulp
Haleakala	a dormant volcano on the island of Maui
haole	foreigner
haupu fern	a large fan-shaped leaf
heiau	a place of worship
Hoku	means 'star', the healer in this story
hula	a dance which tells a story
kahuna	healer
kapu	forbidden
keiki	child
koa	a reddish-brown wood endemic to Hawaii
kona wind	southerly winds

kuma	teacher
lanai	porch
lau hala	a flat-leafed palm
lei	a necklace made from flowers or leaves
luau	a feast, celebration
mahalo	thank you
maile	a deep green leafy vine
Menehune	dwarf size people from the island of Mu
O'pelu	a variety of fish that swim in a school
pili grass	a long-leafed field grass
poi	a smashed up taro root prepared for eating
pua'a	pig
tapa/kapa	the inner layer of bark from the mulberry tree is beaten until it resembles a thin cloth
taro	a starch plant that grows in water
u'hane	Spirit
'umeke	a dried gourd used as a drum
wa'a	canoe, usually made out of koa wood
wahine	woman

About the Author

S. R. BELL, a native of Michigan, moved to the island of Maui, Hawaii in 1989 with her husband and three children at a time when the culture of the Hawaiians and their natural habitat were being threatened by land developers. Many of the water falls, valleys, and mountain trails that she enjoyed with her family are no longer open to the public. Through the Lucy Tuppins' series, Bell reveals a time when the Hawaiian way of life began to change with the influences of western missionary ideals. This is the second of a five part series. Bell has five grandchildren, teaches piano, and is an artist living year round in paradise.

www.srbellmauiwriter.com